The Journey of Jonas Llewellyn

Amanda Aubrey-Burden

Copyright @ 2018 Amanda Aubrey-Burden

All rights reserved

ISBN: 9781980650331

ISBN-13: 9781980650331

Acknowledgments

I dedicate this book to all of the good souls and people who have kept the faith and made this literary journey possible. You all know who you are; family, friends and readers alike – my most heartfelt thanks because it is *your* support that helps keeps the faith in me!

But most of all, I would like to thank Jonas, whose character grew as the story unfolded, and for all the hours he spent patiently guiding me along his journey.
Hopefully his tale will be one of many.

Please note that this is a work of fiction. Names, characters, businesses, places, events, locales, and incidents are either the products of the author's imagination or used in a fictitious manner. Any resemblance to actual persons, living or dead, or actual events is purely coincidental – with the exception of the Dalai Lama, who I hold in the greatest esteem!

The Journey of Jonas Llewellyn

Chapter 1

I was born in a hot, dry country where my ancestors once hunted lions.
Now I hunt ghosts.
The Devil periodically sends forth dark forces in his endless quest to obtain dominance over the earth; it is my job to stop him, and although I am not the only one – know that we walk amongst you, but we are only few.
Such an opening would make for a simpler tale, but nothing is ever as it seems.
I am only one of few, and I was born far away in the land they call Africa – that much is true, but is where the comparison ends.
The dark forces of which I speak are more complex than you could ever imagine, so much so that God, in his infinite wisdom looked out upon a race that would not countenance them, and so it all began.

My name is Jonas Llewellyn; and this is my story...

   I met the man who was to become my father during the famine of 1986. He had come to Ethiopia as many did, to offer what succour he could after experiencing what he referred to as his 'epiphany' and life after that was never the same again.
It is my belief that God has a plan for all of us, and when my mother stumbled into the refugee camp that day with me little more than a babe on her hip, he took one look at her legendary beauty and was smitten on the spot.
We were fortunate, as sadly many were not; for my father-to-be

intended that we would no longer remain there longer than was necessary and made the requisite arrangements to bring us back to Wales.

My mother was at first quite perplexed when this burly ex-miner took her hand and proposed a new life in a far distant land. Having lost my birth-father under mysterious circumstances, the struggle merely to survive since his demise a year earlier meant we had little hope for our future, and it was with an awed sense of gratitude when she finally accepted.

'He is like a gift from God,' she would whisper to me as she cuddled me close in the cold nights, 'and your father would give such a union his blessing, I know, for he was a special man of special lineage as are you, my child. We must trust the greater plan, Jonas, and so I will marry this man and to this new land we will go.'

I have a vivid memory of green hills and a fine mist upon arrival at our new home. How my mother's eyes grew wide at the house and all that lay before us. And how proudly our new benefactor looked on as he showed us the small cottage that sat on the outskirts of the village.

He was, and remains, an exceptional man. Not just because he dared to cross boundaries of culture and colour, but because he genuinely cared for me and took great pains to ensure I was never left out. His love for my mother knew no bounds and steps were taken to adopt me officially. By the time I was two I became Jonas Llewellyn.

That it was an unconventional match and that had caused controversy locally, flowed over my father with no more effect than a Welsh hill fog. But he was fiercely protective of his new-found family and people learned to mumble their opinions far from his hearing lest they invite an impassioned tirade to their small-minded thinking.

Yet there were those who welcomed us warmly into the community, and they would gaze admiringly at my mother's finely-boned features and long braided hair as she walked smoothly among them with all the grace of an exotic black panther.

Her name was Abeba, which means flower, and she came from a long line of African Shamans in Sudan. Tall and willowy she turned heads wherever she went, and as I began to gain in years and height I, too, would attract much attention. This and my colour meant I made few friends but I had little desire to do so, and would read voraciously anything connected to folklore, mysticism and the occult.

Life for me growing up was spent in far-flung lands as I traversed all manner of imaginations of those who had gone before me - and that was exactly how I preferred it. Playing sport or else hanging around the streets held little appeal for me, and as I grew older I developed a deep interest in religion.

My new stepfather, whose name was Rhys, was more than pleased and insisted that he buy me my first bible. As someone who had come to God late in life, he was keen to help me in any way he could. One of my favourite childhood memories was when he would relate biblical stories with such animation I could all but envisage the fall of Jericho, or the angst of Samson. I would curl up next to him before a roaring fire completely entranced by the musical cadence of his rich Welsh tones. He delighted in my interest in religious matters and we would debate endlessly as my mother would look on knowingly a proud glint in her eye.

'You will never win with him, Rhys,' she would say with a soft laugh,' he was born of ancient lineage through his birth-father, may he rest eternally, and his path is well-set. He will be a man of the cloth yet, I don't doubt; but not your usual one.' Then she would throw a sly smile at my father adding, 'A little like yourself as you well know, Rhys Llewellyn ...' and he'd bristle playfully at her.

That there was a genuine love between them was not in doubt. But they were also bonded by something more, something indefinable, and it was only when I was older that my mother tried to explain it to me and how it shaped her decision to leave Ethiopia and place her trust in the hands of a total stranger.

'I saw his kindness as I felt the sincerity of his love,' she told me, 'and the added years he has upon him was not a concern once I realised why our paths had crossed. It soon became apparent to me early on that our future lay with this man.'

'But how?' It was one of my favourite questions to everything, and my mother now gave her slow smile in acknowledgement of this.

'Because your father came to me in a dream and showed me a land beneath the wings of a great dragon and mountains that spread out as far as the eye could see. He was smiling, Jonas, your father was smiling, and I knew then upon waking that our destiny was set and that he had given me his blessing.'

She drew me close so that our eyes were inches apart and there was a serious depth within hers that I had not seen before.

'It is so that you can fulfil your destiny, Jonas, for there flows in you the sacred blood of your ancestors who have always carried the staff of God.' Her voice lowered further and I felt a tremor pass through me. 'Their mission has always been special ... *secret*. You were born for a purpose, named for a path. There are many things in the world that we can never understand, but God's will is never in doubt when he turns his eyes upon you and would have you do his work.'

'His work, mother?' I knew my eyes were as round as the saucers on the Welsh dresser downstairs, but deep within me I could feel something uncoiling as though a great awakening was occurring and despite the gravity of my mother's words I felt strangely calm.

'Do you remember the bad dreams you used to have when you were very small? The faces that would appear in your bedroom wall and how they would sneer and frighten to you?'

I met the steadiness of her gaze and nodded. I remembered them well; the jabbering mouths and distorted faces, the bristling brows and malignant eyes, how they'd curse and babble me as I'd bury myself beneath the blankets in the hope they'd go away.

They did after my mother's intervention when she heard me whimpering one night. I had watched wide-eyed as she swept her arms across the offending faces murmuring sharp words in a strange language.

Afterwards she had come and sat on the bed a small smile on her lips, and seeing the question in my eyes whispered, 'A gift from your father, he shared many of his secrets with me ... now sleep, little one. All is well and there is nothing to fear.' Her manner was soothing and the faces never troubled me again.

As though sharing the memory through my eyes my mother nodded slowly, 'They were not the nightmares of a child, Jonas; those faces were as real as mine and yours. But they were evil faces born of evil beings, low-level spirits back home we'd call *the shetani* ...' she drew back and gazed at me searchingly, 'You understand what it is I am telling you?'

I felt the uncoiling some more and bowed my head.

'*They know you* ... and they will seek to distract and distress you – as they have all those who have come before you. But your bloodline shall not suffer them, or the great evil they perpetually seek to unleash. Trust me; your time will come when all of this will make sense.'

Pulling me into her arms she whispered fiercely, 'But you must never be afraid! Never fear what comes at you from within the darkness, for you are blessed with such light, such *gifts*, Jonas, they will find you are more than a match and your faith will sustain you.'

I felt her heart beating like a war drum as she seemed to draw silently on to something that passed between us like a slow tremor, and I recognised her power momentarily like a flare of a thousand fires and drew breath sharply with the intensity of the moment.

Her eyes when they met mine again were jewelled with tears and I looked at her questioningly.

'Ahhh my son, we are a long way from home; from the land of our birth and fount of our forefathers and as much as I love Rhys who has blessed us with so much, sometimes I cannot help but yearn for the hot touch of the sun upon my skin, to drink in the skies, and hear the language of my people and the songs we used to sing, for it is very different here – but the path, *your* path, remains the same.'

At that strange statement I reached out and stroked the smooth curve of her cheek and she took up my hand swiftly and kissed the palm tenderly.

'Jonas, *my Jonas*, the chosen one, there is no need for such concern in what is a moment of weakness,' and as she smiled her beautiful smile, the tears disappeared like the rains before the sun and once again she was my strong and self-assured mother. 'It is because I know what lies before you and the tasks that lie ahead, but, having spoken much of this with your Rhys – he is as keen as I am that you shall be blessed with every chance to make much of your calling when you are old enough to understand why.'

Leaning in closely she fixed me with those lovely eyes and said earnestly, 'And you will have the choice, Jonas. No one will push you – least of all God, for he knows what terrors abide in the dark and would ask much only of the strongest souls, so know that it will be

your decision and yours alone.
'In the meantime, all we ask is that you apply yourself to your studies and so tell me, Jonas,' her voice had changed, all manner of intimacy now replaced by the usual tones as a mother, 'how fares your time at school? There have been no more problems, I hope?'
She eyed me keenly. School for me had never been easy. Being so dark I attracted the attention of certain bullies, although my height made many of them think twice. One however, was less discerning and there had been an altercation between us with some weeks earlier. But he'd reckoned without the skills of my step-father that he'd passed on to me.

Rhys had been a bare-knuckle champion back in the day and would traverse the valleys fighting for money when he wasn't down the pit.
'I was a hot-head back then,' he'd say with a twinkle in his eye, 'and with a left hook that could fell a man twice my size! My da, God rest his soul, told me straight that if I was going to get into fights after a weekend of drinking then I might as well stay off the beer and get paid for it. And so I did. Ended up going teetotal, too, and made a tidy packet in the process. Not that I'd encourage anyone now to get into that game; but it doesn't do any harm to learn how to defend yourself, Jonas.'
'I would've liked to have met your father ... and your mother,' I'd said somewhat wistfully.
'No, you wouldn't!' The twinkle had become a frown. 'They were both, God bless them, good folk and kindly enough, but they couldn't abide anyone of colour.'
As my eyebrows rose at this, he'd added.
'Aye and they'd have no sooner have welcomed you or your mother through the door as they would a Jehovah's Witness! But I was never of that persuasion despite their prejudice. I was ever a man with my own opinions and I've still enough fight in me should anyone care to tell me any different!'
I could believe it too, he was still powerfully built and had a presence around him that drew respect. It was a shame about his parents, but such discrimination was sadly common and I could only imagine what they might say.
With this in mind he had coached me well in his home-grown way,

before enrolling me into two different martial arts classes and soon I could handle myself with confidence. As a quiet, studious child such exploits were at first abhorrent to me, but as my mother explained on more than one occasion. 'There is nothing to fear, nor is there any shame to be had in the art of empowering yourself as you will see. These children who come against you with their unpleasant ways are but a taste of what really lies out there – and better to be prepared for it; in every way! Besides, you have as much right to be here as any in this country...'
Her tendency to come out with such statements always mystified me a little but when I'd press for more meaning, she'd merely put her finger to her lips and say, 'You'll see.'

And she was right, of course, for by the time I had reached puberty and now even taller nearing over six foot the bullies had melted away, or else tried to inveigle themselves into false friendship, but
I did not have any friends. My quietness made me naturally reserved and I had no interest in anything other than learning and my books. My mother would look on proudly as I bent my head to various texts and my stepfather would sometimes shake his head saying,
'Shouldn't he be out kicking a ball or something? So much study can't be good for him, surely, Abeba?'
My mother would raise her finely-arched eyebrows and reply, 'He does what's in his heart, Rhys. Surely you must know that by now. Let the boy be; he is but preparing his way forward on the path and the good Lord knows best how he should spend his time than us.'
'Yes, I know, *cariad,* but the boy also needs some fresh air once in a while.' Then Rhys would usually appear waggling the gloves at me for a stint on the pads, or else insist I join him for a walk up to the mountains.
I enjoyed these particular excursions immensely for my stepfather was a colourful humorous man who had lived wildly until he'd heard the call from God. Originally from a place called 'Mardy' that lay further up the valley, he had worked below ground as had his father and his father's before him. But the miners' strike and the closure of the pits saw a dramatic change of life for many, and as we'd walk the heights and look down upon the nestling communities, he would

sometimes adopt a mournful look as he'd decry the loss of cultural heritage that had been the life-blood of these parts.
I would wait patiently until the mood had passed before he'd clap me on the back crying, '*Ah, trueni!* But then God has a plan for everything and if I'd still been down the bowels of the pit I would never have met your mother, now would I? Or you, Jonas!'
Sometimes he would fix me with those startling blue eyes and nod knowingly, 'I am as proud of you as if you were my own son, and who'd have thought that I, Rhys Llewellyn ex-collier, once confirmed bachelor, now a man of God, would be stood up on this mountain shouting on the wind and counting out his blessings! Aye.'
Then he might burst into song and sometimes if the mood took me I'd join in. The Welsh, I discovered, loved to sing and 'Sosban fach' was a firm favourite as the sheep around us would pause in their grazing and stare in surprise.
That he loved me like a son, I had no doubt, and although our household was an unconventional it was an extremely diverse and happy one, and soon we were joined by my sister Salome and then two years later by my brother Daniel.
Both were lighter skinned than I and had inherited their father's blue eyes which made them particularly striking and although my mother sometimes sighed for Africa, her every need was taken care of and she was grateful for her life.
Never one to stand idle she'd immersed herself in local affairs and taught evening culinary classes at the local college. She'd even set up a gospel choir that had raised a few eyebrows before pulling in the curious and the brave. My stepfather looked on proudly, a man at ease with himself and happy in his world.

We attended church, of course, where we were often treated to a lively sermon courtesy of Rhys who was a natural preacher and wove stories of everyday struggles that people faced in an increasingly hostile world. He also ran the local community centre and so was always very much in demand amidst the mayhem and the hub of troubled young teenagers and the occasional adult who should know better.
Drugs were a huge problem in our local community, but both parents

were keen for us to be educated about the dangers of them and yet not be exposed, so besides school and attending activities we pretty much kept to ourselves which was helped by living just outside of the village.

My stepfather's parents had passed many years ago, and as the only child he had inherited what had once been an old Drover's inn, although much had been restructured so that it bore no resemblance to its former state besides some dilapidated outbuildings and the old cellar.

A large back garden looked out upon rolling green fields with the mountains in the distance, and it was upon these lofty heights with a stiff breeze blowing in my face that I would sometimes see shapes and figures from the corners of my eye.

I knew them to be shades of the past, one-time inhabitants that still roamed the land as they went about their unseen business. Sometimes they would see me too, and pause in their meanderings and I would find myself staring into curious faces that gazed back at me in confusion, no doubt at finding a black youth amidst their usual haunts.

And haunts there were, and hauntings there were, too. My innate sensitivity was much attuned to the presence by of wandering spirits and by the very nature of my gift they, too, became aware of what my mother called *'my shetani'*.

For the most part their interest in me was fleeting and as insubstantial as their wisps of energy was to me, but sometimes I would sense a whole different feeling that would ripple along the length of my spine as though I was being marked out for special attention, and often I was.

People I would pass in the street would hiss obscenities at me their eyes front, their mouths unmoving which was always a bit perplexing; sometimes I would be thumped in the back or pinched viciously by unseen fingers, and once I woke with faint scratches on my face as though something had attacked me during the night.

My mother became aware, of course, that as I grew older my energies shifted as puberty wrought changes in my body, and that this was very attractive to the darker elements with which we share our world.

It was decided that more help was needed if I was to understand what it was I was up against and protect myself. I was to 'go home'!

This meant a return to Africa so that I could have the benefit of instruction from the elders of my birth-father's tribe. What was left of his kin had remained in Gondar at the foot of the Simian Mountains throughout the famine. That great humanitarian disaster had seen many people misplaced and venture far in search of food, and although I had no memory of this place, or the people, I felt, nevertheless, a deep pulling within as though already they were calling to me.

It was agreed that my father would remain home with the youngest so that my mother and I could visit for four weeks of the summer holidays.

My fellow-pupils at school upon hearing the news of my holiday destination were equally fascinated and at times derogatory in turn, for such exotic trips were unheard of up in the valleys and I was regarded with a mixture of envy and reluctant awe.

'Going back to hunt lions, are you, darkie?' quipped one of my usual tormenters before quickly sidling behind his buddies as I turned my gaze upon him.

For the most part I was blessed with an incredible serenity that seemed to emanate, even when I found myself in the most challenging of circumstances, and it was this inherent lack of fear that I soon learned was to become my most potent and effective weapon - against both the dead and the living.

My fighting skills helped to give me confidence, of course, so I was not such an easy target as many would like, and often you'd see a troop of puny and usually victimised boys following me about the playground smug in the knowledge they were safe with me, and many a time I would intervene with just a look if I saw any of them being tormented.

But the name-calling continued on occasion, albeit from behind a smothered mouth or at a distance, but I hardened my ears and my heart against it as did my mother, knowing that a lack of response often frustrated the antagonists and filled them with confusion.

'There will always be those who will curse us for our colour,' my

mother would say, 'just rise above it, Jonas, and know that their ignorance will revisit them in another form.'
She always had the power to make me feel better and strove, always, to build up confidence in myself and how to conduct myself.
My stepfather was no less willing and gladly spent time helping me understand the narrow-mindedness of certain folk, but it was when I increasingly came under attack by unseen forces he agreed that there were some things beyond even his remit and so the money was found for our air-fare.

Africa; land of my birth, home of my ancestors, cradle of my calling and as we stepped out from the airport and into the heat, its scorching air greeted me keenly like an old forgotten friend.
My mother breathed deeply a bright light in her eyes and squeezed my hand briefly before a man almost as tall as I stepped forward a warm smile on his face and spoke rapidly in a language I was soon to learn was *Amharic*, the ancient tongue of Ethiopia.
With a shriek of pleasure my mother threw her arms around the stranger's neck babbling excitedly before drawing back and pulling me forward her voice suddenly husky with emotion.
'This is he, my eldest child and son of Barak, and the pride of my heart; Jonas, meet your father's brother, Samuel.'
I met the intense gaze of this tall, dark stranger who had a look of me, and having no memory of my natural father felt a kinship nevertheless and a strange lump rose in my throat.
'Ah, how your father would delight in how strongly you have grown,' the man said wonderingly and there too, was a gleam in his eyes, as he reached out and pulled me into an embrace that was as tentative as it was poignant.
'Jonas, it does me good to meet you. We have wondered often how life in a strange country must serve you, but I can see it serves you well, very well indeed. Welcome home, most beloved son of my brother, welcome home!'
As he and my mother talked excitedly he led the way to a dusty sedan parked in the shade of some trees and soon we joined traffic that was on a main thoroughfare despite all of the windows being wide open I soon became sticky with the heat.

My uncle eyed me in the rear-view mirror with just a trace of humour.

'Nothing like the green wet land you're used to, eh, Jonas? Here we can only pray for rain and have relief from the heat. But you will get used to it, and there are robes waiting for you back in the village that will feel far more comfortable.'

I nodded and voiced my thanks, torn between my interest in him and the sights all about us. It felt strange to be here, this land of my birth, and I took in the diversity of it all with an almost reverent respect. Gondar was a mish-mash of fine buildings one minute and tin shacks the next. It was noisy, colourful, bustling, with verdant hills in the distance and the mountains just beyond. I watched as a man skilfully herded his goats among the traffic and inwardly marvelled at the many *'tuttuks'* as they sped and weaved about like blue and white insects vying for business.

Tiny knobby-kneed donkeys pulled at huge loads and my heart pulled for them painfully for I had a deep love for all living things and as though sensing my disquiet my uncle tried to distract me from their plight by pointing out a castle that looked down on the town.

'They call Gondar the 'Camelot of Africa' did you know that, Jonas? We are as rich here in our heritage as once were the emperors who ruled over us! For our land has ever held its sovereignty – despite the wars and the blight of famine...' He paused and exchanged a look with my mother for my father was not the only casualty of that terrible time, and for a moment it was as though ghosts came by and looked in on us with an air of infinite sadness and I suppressed a shiver despite the heat.

Again my uncle seemed to be acutely aware of the shift of my emotions and sought my eyes in the mirror before giving a small nod. 'We are all, from this side of the family blessed with the 'sense' and draw those who have gone before us as does a firefly to a flame. This is why you have come back to us, Jonas, so that we can teach you and show you. It is our scared duty to pass on our knowledge and bind you deep into your destiny with the best chance of success.'

At my quizzical look he added enigmatically, 'Everything has its season.' Then pointing ahead to the mountains he lapsed back into Amharic with my mother and I eased back into my seat as we left the noise and the hubbub behind and the road unfurled before us.

Soon we had left the main road and followed a dirt track grown smooth with use and it meandered into the bush as the landscape about us became more sparsely-vegetated and rocky. Camels munched thoughtfully at the sides of the road as we passed the odd vehicle that would honk its horn in greeting, and besides the dust that perpetually assailed us, the air was rich with a sharp, dry smell as alien to me as was my first breath of Wales when I was a baby.
We were also ascending slowly as the craggy heights drew nearer and nearer, and I was in awe at the raw beauty around me; even my mother had fallen silent as though absorbing the essence of the land. My father's brother began humming softly as we bumped along and soon, through a snatch of trees I espied a cluster of simple round houses with thatched roofs and a lazy spiral of smoke that meandered up to the blue skies.
'Home...' breathed my mother and when she looked back at me there was such delight in her eyes my heart swelled for her evident happiness. She had dreamed of this moment, I knew.
We pulled up alongside an old cart of some sort and a rickety old pick-up and as my uncle killed the engine I heard approaching voices. Into view came what must have been the whole village of some forty people or more with friendly faces full of unrepressed delight. Young children peeped shyly around the adults, but there were none I could see of my age and I knew the reason why.
'Your family,' said Samuel, 'at least some of them are, and they have barely been able to contain their joy since they knew you were coming.'
In a flash my mother was out of the car and disappeared into the small crowd as they gathered around her, voices raised and with much embracing and as though inexorably drawn I, too, alighted from the car and upon seeing me they drew in breaths and fell silent. I moved forward and they parted as like the wind through corn and I came to a halt before them suddenly unsure of what to do. Then they fell on me amidst heart-felt cries in their mother tongue, and over their heads I found my mother's eyes and she was crying.
'Welcome home, Jonas... welcome *home!*'

I felt Samuel's pat my shoulder before he turned away and called for help with our bags and soon we were swept along into the centre of the village before being shown into a large hut where the elders sat waiting to greet us. They were all to a man grey-bearded and simply attired in plain linen robes, but endowed with such an aura of hidden power I hesitated and glanced askance at my mother.
She nodded reassuringly and the welcome party lapsed into respectful silence as Samuel led me forward to be formally presented.
The grey-beards regarded me with especial care as though seeking something deep within *me*, and the air within the shaded confines of the hut became charged with a potent mixture of profound emotion. I felt the weight of every eye upon me as I slowly sank to my knees to receive their blessing.
Kindly voices murmured above my bowed head as I was welcomed into the tribe of my father and then one of them began singing in a quavering tone as the rest of the tribe one by one joined in.
I raised my eyes, my whole being so suffused with love, I felt almost detached from the world as though I was floating, and through the dust motes that danced amidst the shafts of light, I suddenly found myself smiling.

Chapter 2

The next couple of days I spent learning about my heritage and the cultural oddity of my father's people. The official version was that we were of a lost tribe. One of *the* Ten Lost Tribes of Israel, and it was a startling as much as it was fascinating to learn that I was actually of Jewish stock!
But not just any bloodline – an ancient, almost fabled descent from one whose very name would cause no small controversy once the word was out!
I was incredulous. It could not be! *Surely..?*
The Elders impressed on me the need for the utmost discretion. A high call for boy not long into his teens – but then I was no ordinary boy.
I swore to keep the identity of this figure secret until the time was right. But their manner hinted that there was more to my beginnings than they were telling me, and despite my subtle efforts, they would reveal nothing more. It would be some years later on a windswept Isle that I would learn the whole truth and again I would be sworn to silence.
For now, however, this news was enough, and the time I spent with the Elders was an education in itself not least because I had always regarded myself as a child of Africa not of the Holy Land, and as the revelations kept coming, my mind struggled to keep up.
At the first opportunity I spoke with my mother.
'You didn't tell me, you didn't say!'
There was slight recrimination in my tone and she gazed back at me mildly.
'It was not my place. I always knew we would come back and that your ancestry would be made clear to you. But it was not, and you must understand this, ever for me to be the one to tell you, Jonas. And besides, I am not of this tribe, remember.'
'But we are practicing Christians, we go to church! How can this be if I am of a completely different denomination! Mam, I am very confused...'

She laid a hand on my arm.

'Jonas, it's alright, there's no need to fret. I have always told you that your path is different and there are times when one must walk another one – sometimes more than one. It is of necessity that we embrace the religion of Rhys and the Church of Wales, for it is their influence that will lead you to where you need to go.'

I gazed at her in bewilderment.

'Which is where? I still have no idea and small wonder, for everyone seems to speak to me in riddles.'

She lifted her shoulders and we regarded each other silently for some moments.

'So you knew of this, the bloodline of my father? What else do you know?'

'Only that, and very little else. Your father would only confide so much in me, Jonas, but I trusted him as I trust his people, and as you must trust them now. They are your kin and yes, their religious stance is less than conventional, but there are reasons they don't follow the Jewish faith. It has never been their way and it is not my place, nor has it ever been, to question why.'

When I tried to press her further she tapped the side of her nose and turned away.

'If there is more, and I'm sure there is, then let them be the ones to tell you. As I have said, it is not my place.'

I was aware that here were other tribes that claimed Semitic heritage, but most of these had taken up the offer of repatriation in the preceding decades when Israel, together with America, had made it possible for them to return home. Home being the Holy Land, but not to my father's people.

They carved out a living from the land, planting crops, raising livestock, and to all intents and purposes were self-sufficient and at peace with the simplicity of their lives.

I saw no sign of religion while I was there. No prayers, no ritual, no congregation and service or even a holy book. For someone as curious and well-read as I was, it was intriguing.

They had evolved, as a people, into something quite different and had no desire to go to a land they did not know; much less back to a religion they no longer practiced. The Hand of God had guided them

another way as the land had absorbed them along with its secrets, and as much as I yearned to know, my inherent respect for the Elders held my tongue.
What was apparent was that in the preceding centuries the old ways had given way to those much older, and my whole being vibrated with the knowledge with which I'd been given and yet did not fully understand.
Their education of me was as bewildering as it was fascinating. Having been raised conventionally in a church of the Western world, some of the archaic revelations were at odds with what I had been taught and one day, after a particularly intense session I sought out my uncle and gave voice to my fears.
I was worried about what my stepfather might say; he was a deacon and a preacher – how was he going to reconcile our worlds and still have me under his roof? And what of my mother!
The fact she knew all these years and said nothing preyed on my mind. That she had allowed, and actively so, for us to be absorbed into a faith that was fundamentally so different confused me; but then I was just fourteen years old and everything was coming at me so quickly..
Seeing my confusion Samuel smoothed my fears over with all the skill of a man accustomed to such uncertainties.
'It is an intense and disconcerting process, I know, and what makes it more difficult is that you have been so submerged within another culture. But understand this; there are deeper things at work here, there always has been. Do you really think that the man who calls yourself your father would have been allowed near you and your mother if he was anything less than honourable? That either of you would've been allowed to leave here had he been nothing more than a boorish ex-miner who'd heard the call of God? He has been your champion as much as he has been your provider, and yes, he senses that you are different, but he is humble enough to know that there is more to God than praying in a church and reading from a book. So have you no fears there, I tell you. That man came into your life not by accident - and as for your mother!'
He raised an eyebrow as though implying that I should know better.
'Abeba is not a child of yesterday, and knows well the mysteries that

have been revealed to you. Her kin are of an ancient line of Sudanese people well-versed in the arts of medicine and so she flows and she ebbs as she absorbs and changes accordingly. Such are her gifts; the ability to transform and accept, and it is these qualities that allow her to merge with all worlds – as will you, when the time comes. Your mother understands the power of conformity as she does the necessity of assimilating, because therein lies the means of survival in an ever-changing world. Do you understand what it is I am saying, Jonas? '

I thought of my mother and how fully she had embraced her new life as though she had been born to it. Her support my stepfather, the gospel choir, the enthusiasm with which she greeted each and every challenge that came with being a black woman in an often hostile society. As I looked back in that moment I finally understood what it was that gave her such formidable self-assurance. It was the power for survival; taking it, owning it, and holding on tight! And she had done it for both of us.

My heart filled with love as I recognised the sacrifice and how far she had come from her natural heritage. A heritage so culturally diverse only few would understand it.

It explained much and why my father had chosen her to be his wife. She was nothing less than remarkable.

'I hear you, uncle, and yet the Elders swore me to secrecy. It was made plain to me that not even my mother could be in my confidence, and yet you say...'

'That she knows some, yes, but not all. So there is no issue, Jonas, not unless you make it so. The Elders are naturally cautious, we have to be, and your father was ever his own man and he shared more perhaps than he should, but then,' he spread his hands and a small smile played on his lips, 'love wields a strange power and he would've trusted your mother with his life. In turn she has proven more than worthy and she understands. I hope that clarifies things for you.'

It did, in a strange way; she knew, but only *enough*.

Samuel rose and clapped me on my shoulder.

'Now come! That's enough worrying for one day! It has been much to take in, I know, but there is an old African proverb that says 'If you think education is expensive, try ignorance' and so we will not send you ill-equipped out into the world, Jonas. Knowledge will be your most powerful weapon; the rest, as you'll see, will come to you when the time is right. Be content not to push the river.'

With these cryptic words still ringing in my ears we joined the others who were gathering into the centre of the village.

This was my favourite time. Evenings with food and stories around the communal fire where I would gaze at the faces of these folk of ancient lineage and inwardly marvel that I was one of them. That they were different, there was no doubt. There was something in the dark flashing eyes that hinted at something much deeper and I wondered if I channelled the same energy.

My answer came a few days later. After a week of intense study I was informed that Samuel would be taking me up into the mountains to further my training. My heart leapt at the prospect of a change of scenery. As much as I loved learning and my lessons had been fascinating, I longed to see more of this beautiful country and I was equally as keen as my Uncle to embark on the next stage of my journey.

My mother watched proudly along with the farewell party as we took our leave early one morning, the air was still chill and tangy and for the first time in my young life I felt like a man.

By now accustomed to wearing the loose robes of the tribesman, my normal dress and Wales, with its low mists and lush fields seemed like a million miles away as we set off towards the craggy peaks. The sun was rising at our backs as though to see us on our way, and soon we were both sweating as the heat began to rise as we climbed higher and higher before coming to the first plateau where my uncle called for a rest.

As we sipped slowly from our water bottles we also drank in the view, and I felt a thrill of pride run through me for this beautiful land. I knew the mountains of South Wales, of course and had even visited 'Eryri' the Jewel in the Welsh crown once as a boy, but nothing had prepared me for the mountainous vista that unfurled before me for as far as the eye could see. Great rugged peaks set off by wandering green valley's that all but begged to be explored.

To my young mind it was like a 'Lost World', and when I turned to share my thoughts with my newly-found kin it was to find his eyes on me, a small smile playing on the lips.

'I do not have to ask whether you are impressed by what you see,' he said humour in the fine dark eyes, 'for your face speaks more clearly than your tongue ever could," and then sweeping his arm wide he added in a tone more seriously, 'Here have gone many before you in their quest to master the gifts that the good Lord saw fit to bestow upon them; and know that it is an honour that we, of the line of Sheba, once Queen of this ancient land, are graced with such gifts, for not all can bear them and the spirit must be strong. And so I tell you, Jonas...' He broke off abruptly and frowned as his eyes rested on something in the distance.

I followed his gaze and caught movement from the higher slopes as the mountains rose to meet the azure skies, and somewhere deep within me flared that primeval pulsation of 'fight or flight, 'for whatever it was it was travelling at great speed and straight towards us.

'Get behind me! Get behind me, *quickly,* Jonas!'

There was repressed urgency in Samuel's voice and a quiet command and I dived behind him with alacrity my eyes locked on the approaching figure as it raced ever nearer amidst clouds of flying dust, and for the first time in my life I was assailed with a portent of dread and clenched my fists wishing for a weapon.

My uncle stepped forward a few paces, tension in every line of his body as he took up a war-like stance, his staff held before him as I cast desperately about for some means of defence but there were only rocks.

Leaning down slowly, never taking my eyes from the speeding bowl of dust, I gathered a few sharp pieces in my hand and then nearly dropped them as I took in what I saw.

At first I thought it was a large man. But as the brown figure raced towards us I took in the wild hair flying before I realised it was a male baboon - and impossibly huge!

I felt my jaw drop as it howled its fury, bright eyes blazing, the vicious fangs snarling with a terrible intent.

And I froze.

Thankfully my uncle did not, and he leaped towards the beast when it

was just feet away. I watched in disbelief as Samuel seemed to spin up into the air lashing out with the staff so violently I heard the heaviness of the thud as he sent the baboon flying. The creature screeched as it rolled in the dust and my uncle took up another stance as though inviting the baboon in tension in every line of his body.
There was a moment of silence as the beast sought to get its breath, angry eyes fixated on me, the maw open and panting, the great curved teeth still bared with assured promise, and I felt the first stirrings of an emotion that was unfamiliar to me; fear.
The beast rose slowly and shook its great mane and as it drew itself to its full height I was shocked to see that it was well over five and half feet and packed with muscle. The sight of it was as daunting as it was formidable. Did baboons grow this big? And why was it attacking us? A sly look came into the orange eyes as it began to circle my uncle, its focus still on me; and in a flash I understood.
This was no wild beast in the immediate sense; this beast had something *in it* and it had come for *me!*
As I saw the fever in its rabid gaze I suddenly knew what it felt like to be a hunted animal and I remained frozen helplessly unprepared for what would happen next, but Samuel was as intent upon the beast as it was on me, and mirrored its movements like a slow dance of the death, his staff and the calmness of his courage the only things that lay between me and the deadly maw of the beast.
Faint movement in the distance tormented my eye but I could not drag my gaze, nor did I want to, from that of the baboon, and then something extraordinary happened and I found that I *could* see! It was as though I had another eye that rose from the very core of me and in a kind of bemused daze I *watched* with this other means of sight as a flurry of figures approached from the same direction as had come the enraged creature, and my heart dropped like a stone.
It was the rest of the troop, and there were dozens of them. As they charged towards us screeching madly I truly believed in that moment I was going to die.

Time stood still. The sun had suddenly became more intense as though to impress on me that I would soon no longer feel its heat, and the very air around me seemed to whisper ancient secrets as

something woke and stirred within me and I shook off the paralysis because *I wanted to live!* And feeling the stones till in my hands I began to throw them at the charging horde as they dodged and slowed up before coming to an uncertain halt some distance behind their leader that had now paused and was eyeing me malevolently.
The threat was unmistakable and I had never backed down in my life; it was my fight.
'Give me the staff,' I said quietly.
There was just the merest twitch from Samuel to indicate that he heard me his focus entirely on the moment and the added threat of the troop.
'The staff, uncle, if you please ...'
I had moved forward to stand alongside him and still keeping my eyes on the beast I held out my hand and waited.
With deliberate slowness my uncle passed me our only means of defence and in that moment I felt an overwhelming gratitude for his trust as I grasped the wood firmly and stilled my breathing.
The troop were watching me in silence but none more closely than the massive beast as it leered at me making guttural growls deep from within its throat.
It was a challenge and I leaped forward to meet it as all of my years of training kicked in and I lunged at the snarling beast and was rewarded by a sudden uncertainty in its eyes and it pranced back, the maw of it teeth bared even wider as filled with a lightning rage I then began spinning my staff as taught in my martial art classes in a land called Wales, that now seemed like a million miles away. I kept moving forward into the baboon's wake, as it backed up emitting great snorts interspersed with deep growls that belied the confused dawning in its eyes, and it cast about as the troop drew back as though coming to itself.
Then feeling a hand on my back I too, came back into myself as I heard my uncle say my name quietly before coming and standing next to me.
A bird called as it soared overhead as Samuel and I stood shoulder to shoulder.
The great baboon was grumbling still, but the fire had left its eyes and it merely glared as though affronted by our aggressive stance. The

troop had scattered a short way into the distance and were watching keenly as they huddled and clutched at each other, clearly perturbed at events.

With a great show of dignity the baboon gave us a departing bark as it turned and stalked away back to its waiting audience, and I could feel the breath leave my body as the threat passed and I began to shake uncontrollably.

Leading me across to some slabs of rock my uncle bid me to sit as he pulled out a water-skin and put it to my lips, and I gulped almost unconsciously my attention still on the troop as it meandered away, the huge male still casting back the occasional glance.

It was only when they had disappeared up into the higher reaches that my eyes found those of Samuel and they beamed at me with an unmistakable pride as he slapped my shoulder, his face breaking into a delighted smile. Still somewhat suffused with shock I looked at him askance before he threw back his head and emitted a huge guffaw that rose on the air startling a flock of white-billed starlings that had settled on some nearby trees. I wondered if he'd gone mad before I soon found myself laughing along with him, the rumbling of mirth shaking out the shock, and once we were both spent we merely looked at each other as we slowly gained our breath.

'Jonas, I could not have been more proud of you than if you were my own son; and your father, I know, would be dancing a victory dance for the bravery of your display! You did not tell me that you were already in possession of such fighting skills!'

Then he burst into laughter again slapping his knee in sheer delight. My answering smile was a mixture of pleasure, pride and a growing awareness of what I was to become. What I was, w*ho* I was!

I straightened my back and in a rare moment of immodesty savoured the moment.

When my uncle finally gathered himself, he sobered and turned a thoughtful eye on me before saying, 'I can see that your training is not going to be a long drawn out affair. Even a fool can see that you are more than halfway ready. But there is still much to learn and that, was your first introduction to the forces that will be sent against you,' He paused and gave me a quizzical look. 'You know that the attack from the baboon was not of its choosing, don't you? That there was something else driving the beast and that made it the size it was. There have not been baboons that size around here in thousands of years. It was a powerful display and you got the better of it - this time! But don't let it go to your head. Never let your guard down, not for one minute, for the dark forces will use whatever means necessary to turn you from your path'

I nodded.

'Yes. I have seen them before – but nothing like this. I thought it was going to *kill me!'*

'And it would have, too, Jonas. Make no mistake about that. But it has served as a warning and so we will remain vigilant. Come,' he gave me another slap on the shoulder. 'The cave is not far, and then we can begin your training in earnest.'

As we scrambled and climbed ever higher I kept a keen eye on the landscape around us but nothing moved in the distance or appeared to be following us, yet for some unknown reason I felt as though our every movement was being watched.

The sun beat down relentlessly and repeatedly I wiped the sweat from my brow as our sojourn took us even higher. But my uncle seemed unfazed with the heat and led the way forward purposely, and it was with no small sense of relief when we reached another plateau he turned to me saying, 'We are here!'

I sank down on to my haunches as I caught my breath and then lost it again as I took in the views all around us; it was like being on top of the world and I could feel my eyes widen with wonder.

'It is quite something else, isn't it!' declared Samuel proudly, 'and for all of your mountains in Wales, I am sure they do not come as close to heaven as this.'

I could not disagree with him as through the haze I gazed down at the verdant valleys that spread out below us. It was almost surreal, like looking at a painting, my sense of being was so detached and I was glad to sit quietly for several minutes as my mind reconnected itself and my breathing returned to normal.

My uncle was watching me closely and after a while I stood up feeling more steady and favoured him with a boyish grin.

'My father back home would not have the same opinion, I'm sure, for the Welsh love their mountains as they do their country but,' and I nodded slowly, 'I'm also of the mind he would appreciate such a sight as to take it to his grave and gladly.'

'Why, Jonas!' my uncle returned with a chuckle, 'you are quite the old man and with a poem in your heart.' And I felt myself grow hot with embarrassment.

'It is this place. These mountains...'

He waved a hand before turning away but not before I caught sight of the pleasure in his face.

'No, Jonas, son of my blood; you are simply becoming who you are. Look, see that cleft in the cliff? That will be our home for the next two weeks!'

I followed as he led the way across the uneven ground towards a narrow opening that was partially hidden by some scrub. Samuel pushed it aside and beyond lay a cool dark interior the size of a large hut and to my surprise, it was well-provisioned along with two sleeping pallets with kindling and wood stacked up in the far corner for a fire.

'A cave ...' I breathed delightedly before a sudden thought occurred to me, 'and the baboons?'

'No need to worry yourself, Jonas. They'll know it's here but they can't come in.' my uncle's tone was matter-of-fact and I looked up at him questioningly.

Again that enigmatic smile.

'All in good time, Jonas, all in good time...'

After we'd washed the dust from our faces and partaken off some water, Samuel showed me where everything was and offered me the choice of bed.

'How is this all here in the first place?' I asked as Samuel removed some fruit and began to peel it with lighting dexterity.

'We have used this place for centuries,' he told me, 'and we keep it well stocked at all times, as our forebears did before us. It is a sanctified place that can't be breached – not even by wild animals. It is a *special* place, Jonas, for it is here that we take on the mantle that has been gifted to us, come, we will sit outside and find some shade.'

Bearing a platter each we each took a seat beneath a nearby tree and looked out across the heat haze as the mountains marched all around

us.
That it was a special place I had no doubt. There was an air of otherworldliness about our whole surroundings that spoke of something inherently ancient and sacred, and as I passed the sweet fruit between my lips I felt suitably humbled.

We spoke for the remainder of the afternoon – or rather my uncle spoke and I listened, and it was only when he rose and stretched some hours later that I realised the sun was dipping beyond the horizon and I shivered in the sudden coolness of the air.
Leaning down my uncle extended a hand and drew me to my feet.
'It gets cold in these mountains at night, but fear not, my young warrior, for we will soon have a fire going and there are plenty of blankets within to keep us warm.'
As I fed the fire my uncle soon had a pan filled with a spicy smelling stew made up of different vegetables before moving onto preparing the *'injera'*.
'You will have to forgo your taste for meat whilst you are on this journey, Jonas,' he told me placing a skillet on to the cooking stand above the flames. 'The essence of animal parts will interfere with the absorption of natural energies, so your diet shall be as of those who have come before you. No meat, of any kind, and that includes fish.'
He flashed me a quick smile, 'It is not so bad and you will soon feel the benefits, I promise you.'
'What...for *always?*'
'For always. You'll get used to it!' His tone brooked no argument and inwardly I frowned.
This was something else my mother had not seen fit to share with me, and I absorbed this new instruction with mixed feelings. My mind flashed to the huge Sunday Roasts my stepfather would insist on cooking and how he might react to this new development! But as Samuel had said, Rhys was canny enough to understand that this was *my* journey, not his, and that if meat was to be removed from the menu for me, then so be it.
We ate in silence with just the crackling flames of the fire for company and there was between us an easy air, and inwardly I marvelled at finding myself in this place and with a growing

excitement for what more discoveries would lay ahead.
When our meal was finished and the plates wiped clean, my uncle went over to the cave opening and gestured that I join him. Huddled in my blanket for the air was quite chill beyond the fire I did as I was bid, and pointing up to the sky he simply said, 'Look.'
I gazed up into the night skies and took in a long inward breath as the heavens spread out before us ablaze with the most beautiful sights known to man.
'I have seen many stars.' I breathed wonderingly, 'But I never knew there could be *so many!*'
As the canopy of brilliance twinkled for a far as the eye could see, I sensed a swift change in my uncle's attention and followed his gaze into the darkness from whence came an unmistakable light of another kind and my pleasure was instantly arrested.
'There's no need to be afraid, Jonas,' Samuel murmured, 'He cannot come in.'
I worked saliva into the dryness of my mouth before I could make a reply.
'But what is he... *it* doing here?' although deep inside me I knew the answer.
The night-shine of the male baboon eyes stared back at us unflinchingly as it sat on an elevated piece of rock some thirty yards away, and I felt its glare upon me like a malevolent spirit of the night.
'You are obviously of great interest and regarded as a threat; but then so was your father and he was stalked by a mountain lion, so you might want to count yourself fortunate!'
The soft chuckle that followed on from this statement saw me drag my gaze from the silent sentinel and look my uncle in shocked awe.
A mountain lion! *My father?'*
Samuel nodded.
'Come,' he said turning away, 'the beast will be held at bay for it cannot enter,' He hunkered down by the fire and threw more sticks on the fire, 'besides, the time is right to speak now of your father. Your journey has already started and it is only fair you know what else to expect.'

Chapter 3

I needed no further persuading. The insidious stare of the creature that stood guard unnerved me and I was also keen to learn more of my birth father.
His presence in my life had been short and fleeting and I had no memory of him other than a rich laugh and a touch that soothed me. My mother had spoke of a giant amongst men, for he had been extremely tall and powerful with it, but he was mortal, nevertheless, and even giants have been known to fall and how I had wished, often, to have known him.
And so casting a final look at the watching beast I returned to the warmth of our inner sanctum and sat down and waited for my uncle to speak.
'There is much sorrow in our world and much darkness; so it has always been, and so it will always be until he who was once Lucifer tires of the struggle, or else is struck down.'
A shower of sparks rose dramatically as though in situ with his words and I found my eyes grow wide.
'Lucifer!'
Samuel gave a grim smile.
'The Devil, Satan, The Dark One, call him what you will, but he is not, as some would have it, some being conjured up from myth. He's with us, in whatever form he can master, and enlists, continually, lost souls and those not strong enough to withstand his wiles. Seems hard to believe he was once the most beloved of all God's angels, and yet he seeks only to destroy all that is good.' A ripple of sadness crossed the handsome features and he paused before adding, 'And he got your father in the end.'
I drew back perplexed but somehow managed to find my tongue.
'But mam said ... my mother told me that he died of starvation! That he died during the famine!'
My uncle fixed me with a steady gaze for some moments before answering.
'He did die during the famine that much is true. But not of

starvation.'

I felt a creeping reluctance steal over me for I suddenly had an urge *not to know*.

The flames crackled between us that set shadows dancing all around the cave and the air itself seemed to grow still as though listening.

'We had left the village in search of food; word had come that there was an Aid delivery several miles away, and so we set out, your father and I. With us also came two of our cousins. Everyone was weak with hunger but we believed we had strength and faith enough to make the journey. God was watching over us for indeed for we made it to the Aid camp and rested briefly before setting off with supplies for the village; and that was when we met the man on the road.'

Samuel paused staring beyond me as though looking back to that day and then seemed to gather himself.

'He was in great distress and was little more than a bag of bones in rags. He was also half-mad with grief. Said that he'd had to leave his wife some miles back in the bush, that she was heavy with child and could go no further, so he had set out to seek help and, your father...well ...' My uncle threw me a poignant look, 'being the man he was, insisted we go on ahead and that he would go in search of this woman. He was equally insistent that we take the man with us and give him succour. And we, against our better judgement agreed, for there was something about the fellow I did not like, but there was no arguing with your father when he set his mind to something and besides, hunger and heat does things to a man and we were all of us, keen to get back and out of the sun.'

He poked at the fire and sent a shower of sparks dancing.

'It was the last time I saw him. He set out across the wasteland with just a skin of water and nothing other than noble intent, for to have turned his face away from the stricken would be to deny his soul, and like those who had come before him, his calling was strong.'

A silence fell between us as I absorbed these words and my uncle gazed once again into the past, and after some moments I ventured to ask, 'What happened to him?'

Samuel gave a sad smile.

'What usually happens to those drawn down the path of deceit; he

walked into the wilderness never to return. There was no woman. It was a trap. He perished in the desert. Even for all of his fighting skills, he was heavily outnumbered and sadly he was taken down.'
I stared at him in shock, barely able to believe my ears.
'But how, how do you know this?'
'There were signs...bloodstains and marks of a great struggle. That he had fought bravely there was no doubt, but he was already weakened by hunger and the heat of the desert is no place for a man, even one who was as singular and as blessed by God as your father was and, well ...'
'So they killed him!'
My tone was harsh, my voice thick. Samuel met the anger in my eyes with a profound sadness of his own and lifted his shoulders.
'But what? *Who,* Uncle? What took his life?'
'We do not know for sure. We never discovered exactly what happened that day; only that your father was taken, and we never set eyes on him again.'
I drew back. It was almost too much to take in. The man whose seed had brought me into the world, the man who was my father, *my father*, the love of my mother's life, the man whose blood ran through my veins brought down in the desert like a wild beast! I felt a lump rise in my throat.
'How did you know... how did you know it was him? You said there were signs.'
My uncle stood up and then went to the back of the cave. He retrieved a long shape wrapped in a length of fine linen and then brought it across and held it out to me.
I stared at him and then at the mysterious gift that was being offered, and seeing my hesitation Samuel nodded.
'Take it.' He said quietly.
I reached out and took the wrapped bundle tentatively into my hands and something passed through me.
My uncle returned to his place and waited his face enigmatic.
With a great care I unwrapped the length of cloth before drawing out a smooth length of wood that seemed to hum in my hands and I looked up to the dark eyes watching me.
'My fathers..?'

Samuel bowed his head.

I ran my hands along the length of wood and was suddenly overcome by an emotion I could not explain. I clasped it to my chest and gave a great shudder.

'Your father came to me in a dream that night, Jonas. He told me to go and retrieve the staff and where to find it. He also bid me beware the man we had found on the road for he was not who he purported to be. Upon waking I immediately went to check on the strange traveller but of course he had gone and I knew then, that your father had met an ill end.'

We regarded each other with an intensity that seared me to the bone but I held back the tears that threatened to unman me and dared to ask another question, although inwardly I already knew the answer.

'So this ... man, this stranger, was like the baboon that sits outside now waiting for me?'

'Yes, in a way,' Samuel replied quietly, 'although the baboon is as much the puppet as was the man we met on the road.' He leaned forward, 'Jonas, know that the Beast has taken centuries to perfect his craft and can take on many forms. He can disguise himself and take on all manner of beings in his bid to secure a foothold in this world. And some people, being what they are,' he raised his shoulders, 'well, they are often at the mercy of their weakness and when the Devil sets the lure, they can no sooner resist that can a wild animal that knows no better.'

'Hasn't he secured enough!' I burst out in sudden anger and saw my uncle's eyebrows rise in surprise, then the tears came, hot and heavy as they ran down my cheeks and I dipped my head with shame.

'Fear these emotions not, Jonas, for by their expression you honour your father and the bravery of his heart with the acknowledgement of yours. Know also that he is beyond suffering now and no doubt watches over you, as he has always watched over you. The darkness may have claimed his life, but it had no claim on his soul - and so he lives on, somewhere, forever in the light, but to answer your question; no, the Darkness will not stop until it claims every man, woman and child. And so it has ever been.'

Silence fell between us again as I considered his words and allowed myself to feel a sense of grief for a man I had never known, and when

I raised my eyes it was to find my uncle watching me closely.

'I wish I could have known him. I wish I had some memory of him and could put a face to his name. But where was God in all this? Why did he allow my father to die? ' My voice was soft, wistfulness having replaced the flare of anger. It just all seemed so pointless, the waste of a life and a terrible end. For the first time in my life I felt the foundations of my faith move beneath my feet but I had to *know,* I *needed* to understand!

Samuel stacked more wood on to the fire before making his reply.

'God has his hand in this world, but we all also have ours, and your father made a decision that day that cost him his life, despite all attempts to dissuade him. So you see; God was looking out for him, Jonas, through me and my words of warning. But he heeded them not, and I could not stay him. No one could, and yes, his thinking was weakened by hunger and the famine, for daily survival was a struggle to us all, but he made his choice in the spirit of honour, and being your father, I would have expected nothing less.'

I was not expecting such a simplistic answer and I mulled it over for some moments before venturing, 'So he put the life of an unknown woman before that of my mother ... and me?' there was a petulant tone to my voice that I hated, but I couldn't help myself.

For the first time I saw anger flare in my uncle's face as he leaned towards me and I shrank back in awareness of having caused offence.

'Boy, all lives matter! No one is of no consequence in the eyes of God! And yet you have a childish view of the world,' the ire died in his face a suddenly as it had come, 'but then you have only been taught one way and have much to learn of life and how the mysteries work. We will have much to discuss and there will be much that will become clear during our time here.'

He nodded towards the staff.

'That belonged to your father,' he said quietly, 'and his father before him, and his father, and so on,' He smiled suddenly all sternness dispelled, 'Jonas, dwell not, on the passing of your father, nor feel that he went like a lamb at the end. For when we went out the next day to search for him, we found not his remains, but we did the site of his last stand and the bones of at least half a dozen men. The hyena's had been busy in the night but I can tell you without an iota of doubt that those of your father were not among them. We found only his staff and for that, we must be grateful for small mercies, for it is no ordinary staff, Jonas.'

I stared at him and then down at length of smooth wood I had laid back at my feet.

The fire crackled and spat as though the tongues of flame were frustrated in their attempts to speak and break the silence

'What's so special about it? I don't understand.'

Samuel began to bank up the fire with heavier bits of wood that would smoulder through the night. 'You will,' he said eventually, 'the answer lies in what is before you, so take the time to acquaint yourself for it yours now and in the morning I will show you its hidden powers.'

Tentatively I reached out and took the staff back into my hands. It was finely-grained and seemed to hum as my fingers caressed the smooth length before finding a series of small joins in the wood. I looked up at Samuel questioningly.

'In the morning, Jonas, in the morning ... Come, it has been a long day and so it shall be tomorrow. Let us sleep now with the hope our dreams will be sweet.'

At this remark the question I had been harbouring amongst many came to my lips and was out before I knew it.

'Uncle, did you ever see my father again after that night? In a dream, I mean ...' and felt my heart sink as Samuel shook his head.

'I'm afraid not, Jonas Even his image that night was shadowy and not strong, but his words were enough to give warning and guide us to where he'd made his stand.'

'His last one..?'

We gazed at each other, conjoined by a strange kind of grief.

'So it would seem.' He concurred quietly.

There was nothing more to be said.

I drew myself into the make-shift bed and on impulse pulled the staff in with me. I could feel my uncle's eyes upon me but I didn't care. This was the closest I was ever going to get to my real father, and it gave me no small comfort.

Samuel leaned across and extinguished the lamp and the cave came alive with jumping shadows and I started up as a snarl suddenly came out from the darkness outside.

'Fear not, Jonas, he cannot come in,' said Samuel unconcernedly as he wrapped himself up in his blankets. 'As I have told you, this place is protected and if you are to succeed and stay safe in the path that's been chosen, then the first lesson is to trust those around you who have your best interests at heart. Now relax and go to sleep; no harm will come to you this night,'

Gingerly I lowered myself down onto the crude bed still holding my father's staff and pulled the blankets around me my eyes riveted to the mouth of the cave and almost absentmindedly murmured, '*Nos da.*'

'What?'

My uncle shifted and regarded me through the glow of the firelight his expression almost comical and I found a small smile.

'It's Welsh, it means 'good night,'

'Ahhh, I see,' and he returned my grin, '*Nos da*, it is then,' and in that shared moment of almost normality I felt a calmness come over me and settled down to sleep, the staff held closely as the shadows around me slowed in their dance, and soon my eyelids grew heavy as the exertions of the day took its toll, and I slipped into a deep sleep my last thoughts of a brave man who had given his life for a woman who didn't exist.

Some time later I woke suddenly to find the cave almost in complete darkness, the fire was just a smouldering pile of twinkling ashes and yet there was a luminescence just out of sight that drew my eye, and turning my head slowly I clutched the staff tighter as my gaze traversed the sleeping form of my uncle and found its way to the cave entrance where stood an impossibly tall figure that glowed like the palest flame and my heart came to a stop.

It was a man, and yet the face was extraordinary with eyes of the lightest hue. He was looking at me with just the merest hint of a smile, and then the handsome features broke into a smile and he bowed his head as though in acknowledgment before turning to gaze out back into the night - and then he was gone.

I blinked several times and raised myself on to my elbow looking about wildly.

The strange light had disappeared plunging the cave into total darkness but I could just make out Samuel as he slept on oblivious. I had seen many things in my time but it was the first time I'd seen an angel. *An angel!*
I lay back down. So it was true! Such celestial beings did exist, and for the first time since coming to this hot, arid land I felt safe.

Chapter 4

When I woke the next morning it was to find the fire relit and Samuel stood at the cave mouth and as the memory came flooding back, I dispensed with the usual morning greeting and cried, 'I saw an angel! *I saw an angel last night, Uncle!'*
'Ah, so you are finally awake,' he said smilingly.
'Yes, and I saw one, *I saw one*, I tell you!'
My uncle laughed and coming back to the hearth and poured some water into a pot ready for boiling.
'And did he speak ... this angel?'
I watched him as he began to make up the dough for our breakfast as I formulated my thoughts. Now that I was fully awake it seemed almost like a dream and I hesitated before I made answer.
'Well, no, he didn't say anything. He was just stood over there where you were, staring at me.' Then a thought suddenly occurred to me. 'You just said *he*...I didn't say the angel was a *he* just that I saw an angel...'
I trailed off feeling slightly foolish for having so readily indulged my younger self in my excitement and I cleared my throat self-consciously. It probably was a dream brought on my last night's conversation and wishful thinking, but then my uncle surprised me by saying.
'Well, doubtless that's because I see him all the time, for *he* makes it his business to visit often, Jonas,' he paused in the action of flipping the *injera* and gave me a small smile, 'and so it was only a matter of time before he would make himself visible to you.'
I sat up and drew the blankets around me closely; there was still a nip in the air as I stretched my toes out to the welcome heat of the fire as I processed this latest revelation.

'He comes to visit you? You see him often?'
'Of course. He is the guardian who protects this cave.'
I fell silent, in awe at the matter-of-fact way Samuel made this statement, and as I opened my mouth to ask another question he gave a nod to the opening saying,
'It is safe to go out and make water. Your friend, the baboon will have returned to his troop and is no doubt partaking of some breakfast of his own. There are towels over there, so rouse yourself, Jonas, there is much we have to do for the time we are here and every moment is precious.'
As I stumbled out into the chilled air I looked about me warily. There was no sign of our night-time watcher, but I hastened with my ablutions anyway as the sun rose steadily to reveal a breathtakingly beautiful dawn, and for the briefest of moments I felt a pulse of *hiraeth* for the green hills of what was now my home.
But camping out in the wilds of Africa was the kind of adventure every boy my age could ever dream of and I found myself wondering what my school friends would say if they could see me now. Or even my stepfather and siblings for that matter, and I pinched myself because everything was so exotic and different there were times that even I found myself stunned into wondrous disbelief.
Unbidden came into my mind the images of narrow tiered streets, drizzly mornings where mountains hid behind mists and how the people went about their business in vibrant musical voices. I envisaged our cosy cottage set against the backdrop of the curve of green hills and heard the loud ticking of the clock in the parlour, and as an eagle soared high amidst the thermals, its lonesome call suddenly brought me to myself and I hurried back to the cave.

Breakfast complete and the dishes wiped cleaned, Samuel took up his staff and indicated I do the same and as I went to pick up one of the spare ones that was stacked to the side my uncle shook his head.
'No, take up your father's one, Jonas. You have no need for a boy's staff now.'
With mixed feelings I did as I was bid and followed him out into the brightness. Already the heat was rising but we struck out briskly along the plateau, Samuel leading the way with his long, easy stride.

Soon we were in a large shaded area beneath an outcrop of rock and then my uncle threw off his robe and turned to face me. For the purpose of such a session my uncle was wearing a loincloth and now assumed a war-like stance, his staff braced before him.

'Come on, Jonas; don't be shy with me now. Your mother tells me you have been busy all these years learning how to master the art of defence and attack, and if you think yesterday's experience was the worst it's going to get, then know now that that was nothing.' He jerked his head at me, 'Yesterday you fought a wild animal, today you fight a man. Come! Let's see what you can *really* do!'

I gazed at him in perplexity, for not only was he twice my size but he also had years of skilled experience and I shuffled my feet uncertainly.

'Jonas, cease your dithering! Have faith in your abilities and in those your father has given to you'

Unsure of what the last part of his directive meant I pulled my robe over my head and stood lamely in just my underpants feeling rather foolish, but my uncle was relentless.

'Take up your staff, boy, and let's go to it!'

He made a few movements towards me and instinctively I assumed a defensive position as then something remarkable began to happen. It was as though I became a part of the staff I now held out before me, and as my uncle came at me again it was as though the length of wood sprang into life and I feinted then swung as Samuel jumped back before coming at me again and I dipped and struck as to my horror my uncle's legs flew up into the air and then he was suddenly sprawling in the dust!

I stepped back and then forward unsure what to do next as then came to me the unmistakable laughter of my father's brother as he sat up wiping the tears from his eyes before regarding me in amusement.

'Don't look so mortified, Jonas that was better than I thought! Indeed, by all that's holy, that was superb!'

'What ... what do you mean?'

But I did feel mortified, no matter his words and glanced at the staff as it seemed to hum quietly in my hands. Or was I imagining it? The exposure to so many different feelings and experiences falling fast on the heels of each other had me questioning my senses, but I then had my answer with my uncle's next words.

'Jonas, your father's staff is more than a weapon. It is made from a sacred wood from the Thyia tree, as I told you. Honed and shaped by the hands of your ancestors who have also walked the warrior's path on which you find yourself. The staff has been blessed and made stronger still by all those who have used it, and now you have just seen its power and yet it more than that again. Here, let me show you.'

Effortlessly he leaped to his feet and held out a hand for the staff and feeling as though I was losing a part of myself, reluctantly handed it over.

'Ha, already I see by your face you have bonded! But have no fear, Jonas; you shall soon have it back. Now watch,' His fingers indicated the delicate crevices I had found the previous evening and within a few swift movements the staff became a cross. Then he executed a sudden movement and the cross became a staff once more and I had to stop my mouth falling open.

'How ... how did you do that?'

My uncle demonstrated again before handing me the staff and after a few tries I had soon mastered it and then shook my head wonderingly.

'It as though it is alive, Uncle,' I said in an awed undertone, 'I can *feel* it, I swear, as though it is *talking* in my hands!'

'And so it is,' replied Samuel and patted me on the back, 'and has much to teach you. I am just the facilitator, Jonas; this is your *real* teacher. And the more you work with it and listen to it, the more you will know, the better you will become, and the faster you shall grow in the gifts that God had already bestowed on you.' He nodded knowingly, 'Such power men can only dream of. But we are of the very few entrusted with this special path, and all knowledge of what you need to know is within this very staff. The Thyia from which it is made has always been sacred - it is The Tree of Life after all. Indeed the wisdom of its wood goes back a time when the *jinn* were considered all-knowing.'

The jinn?

I creased my brow at him. There was so much to take in and seeing my look he cried, 'Come! Enough talk! I will explain more to you later. Let's see what else you can do, my young warrior!' and with that he gave me a playful dig in the ribs before springing back and soon we were engaging in a kind of combat that was not familiar to me and yet felt strangely natural, and the rest of the morning passed in a blur of defence and attack, parry and thrust, as the staff sang and swept through the scorching air and the sweat ran freely from us both. My uncle would call for brief but frequent breaks as we'd catch our breath and take sips from the water-skin, and by the time the sun was at its zenith, the shadow had receded and we moved to a different spot where we rested and ate fruit looking out across the valley.

'Your reflexes are fast but at times I have seen you hesitate when such indecision could be your downfall,' said my uncle and spat out the stone from a peach, 'pain can be our greatest teacher but you must not wait for it, Jonas. Trust in the guidance of the staff, for it will protect you in two ways, and believe me when I tell you there is much out there you will need protecting from.'

We sat in silence for some moments before I ventured. 'These beings, these *jinn* of what you speak. Are they like the *shetani* my mother has told me about?'

'Yes, they are similar, but not the same. The *jinn* are of sacred descent and a supernatural energy of which flows through your veins.'

I glanced at him startled and he gave a small nod.

'Yes, but it is nothing to be frightened of, and better for you to embrace it. *Shetani* is of a lower caste of spirit and not to be trifled with. They are malevolent and unfriendly and will seek only to cause you disruption.'

I thought of the faces I used to see in the walls of my bedroom as a child and felt I understood.

'So it was the *shetani* that was in the baboon and possessed the men that killed my father ...'

It wasn't a question and Samuel saw fit to make no answer. We fell into silence, each with our thoughts.

Everything that was being revealed to me I accepted with an ease that surprised me. It was like the a piece of the world had been peeled back and I had been given a glimpse of what lay below, and as I was greeted with each new insight, my mind merely expanded further as I took it all in. I turned my gaze up into the sweltering skies and sent a silent prayer to God for his great blessing and then looked gratefully to my uncle.

'You have been so good to me - like a father. I hope one day I can give something back ... to *all* of you. I have never been made to feel so welcome.'

He gave me a long look.

'It cannot be easy being so different in such a different place. When your mother told me she was leaving to marry this man and start a new life, we were concerned, naturally, but if you were to survive that terrible time and fulfil your destiny, you had to be given the best chance,' he paused and looked out across the ragged tips of the mountains and shook his head, 'You would not remember, being so small, but those of us who could make the journey to the camps had done so, little knowing what fate awaited any of us – least of all you and Abeba. God works in mysterious ways, Jonas, for here you are delivered back to us, and so much like your father at that age it is as though the years have never been, and I see in your eyes the same spark that will serve as a light for the dark days ahead.'

'Dark days?' I turned and met his stare squarely.

He rose to his feet with all the grace of a panther and then drawing me to my feet said, 'No need to worry about that now. One thing at a time, my young warrior, and for now I am about to show you your first opening moves of *Kalaripayattu*. It is the most ancient form of combat and with your existing knowledge of martial arts I am confident you will pick it up very quickly.'

And so passed the next couple of weeks as the days fell into a pattern of training and exercise and as my fighting skills improved so did my confidence. As we ate and rested in between we talked as I was wove a picture of what I was to expect, and having seen no sight nor sound of the baboon since that first night it was with a shock that I found it blocking my path as I returned one morning with water from the spring and my first thought was *shetani!*

It regarded me balefully with its amber eyes and peeled its lip back slowly to reveal the deadly fangs and I knew in that moment that this would be no opportunistic tussle and I would have to fight for my very life.

Chapter 5

Slowly I lowered the container of water to the ground as I kept my eyes riveted on the beast. It bared its teeth further in a crazy rictus-smile, and I could smell the rank musk of its tangled fur. Aware that I had no weapon to protect me now, every hair rose on my body as deep from within the great maw came a blood-curdling snarl.
We stared at each other, its orange eyes intent upon me, my mind beginning to race at this unexpected sight.
Stay focused, Jonas, I told myself, *it's just a bad spirit.*
I eased in a long deep breath and stepped back slowly.
The baboon, mistaking my retreat for weakness came at me with a speed that was frightening and it was more luck than skill that saw me spin out of its path as it lunged wildly at where I'd been standing. Keen not to lose the surprise of the moment I leapt up and kicked with all of my might and had the brief satisfaction of seeing the great beast go sprawling into the dust
It shook its head, dazed for a moment before leaping at me again its eyes wild with an infernal fire and I caught its foul breath as it snapped and lunged just inches from my face. With no staff to defend me my whole body came alive in one powerful fluidic movement as all of the training kicked in as I blocked and dodged and blocked again the grappling arms and leering teeth.
The baboon's attack was relentless, and I could feel the sun scorching the sweat on my back as the heat sapped insidiously at my strength, and I wondered how long I could keep it up. I heard a shout and became aware of something coming towards me and fast, but I didn't dare take my eyes from the beast as thankfully the third one that lay hidden suddenly flared into life.
With this sense rather than sight, I saw my father's staff sailing towards me like an arrow of truth and felt a surge of triumph as I reached up and snatched it from the air!
This action appeared to inflame the creature further and it came at me with renewed effort. But I was now infused with the power of an ancient magic and went forward fearlessly, the staff lightening fast in

my hands.
It soon became apparent that if the baboon couldn't have me then it would take the staff. It grabbed repeatedly constantly changing the tactics of the fight, and at one point we wrestled furiously, its snapping jaws a hairsbreadth from my throat its breath hot with fetid rage.
To my horror I felt the staff yanked between us as the beast broke through my defences and somehow I managed a manoeuvre that released the beast's grip and it rolled a few times before jumping to its feet screeching furiously. Then to my astonishment, I watched as it grabbed up a fistful of dirt as it came at me slowly, the orange eyes glinting slyly, the fanged mouth gaping with vicious intent, and I realised the danger for if it succeeded in blinding me, even momentarily, then those teeth would be on me in an instant.
I backed up slowly and it followed never taking its eyes from my face, and I felt the first stirrings of fear. It wasn't simply the fact I was grappling with a wild animal that was frightening, as knowing what was in it and the fierceness of its intent.
Then I heard my uncle's voice and even amidst the rising panic of my emotions I was wondered how he had got behind me. And as the beast drew nearer emboldened by my retreat I heard words almost like a whisper and so close to my ear it was as though Samuel was stood right next to me.
Have no fear, Jonas.
Then in clear quiet tones he gave me an instruction.
I heeded it and without further ado lashed out at the baboon with a yell of defiance, and before it could unleash the dust into my face I heard a loud crack as the strong muscularly arm snapped. There was a high-pitched scream that rebounded around the mountains and then I saw my uncle come running from *behind* the beast, but there was no time to wonder as I saw him raise a spear and draw back his arm.
'*No!*' I shouted and Samuel skidded to a stop. 'Let him go!'

We watched as the beast wheeled and scarpered across the rock-face still howling, its broken limb dangling and I felt pity for it despite its virulent attack on me.
Samuel moved swiftly towards me his hands held up in a questioning

gesture and I shook my head.
'I'll not have the blood of that beast on my hands.'
'But, Jonas, he is no cuddly ape with which you will one day make friends! It would rip your face off as soon as look at you!'
He was disgruntled I knew, but already I was feeling my power and my inner direction, and I would not kill any living creature possessed or otherwise - not if I could help it, and besides, as I had been told so many times, my path would shape as *I* would want it.
My face must've changed because he peered down at me concernedly.
'Are you alright? No, I can see you are not. It is the shock. Here, put your arm round my shoulder and let's get you inside. I'll come back for the water.'
A sudden trembling had taken hold of my body and I felt light-headed as my legs turned to water and as soon as Samuel helped me into the coolness of the cave, I slumped gratefully on to my pallet until the shaking had begun to subside.
Thrusting a piece of fruit into my hands my uncle commanded me to suck out the juices.
'The sugar will help with the shock,' he told me and then disappeared outside to retrieve the water canister.
By the time he returned I was feeling much better but he gave me time to come fully to myself as he made preparations for our evening meal, and as soon as I felt my voice wouldn't betray me, I spoke.
'I think I have just had my real first fight with a *shetani*.'
Samuel raised his eyebrows as he spooned rice mixed with vegetables on to our plates.
'And defeated it, although why you wouldn't let me finish the job I don't know,' he handed me a brimming plate, 'although I doubt very much it'll be back you will have done it no favours by letting it live, I'm telling you.'
'Why?' I asked and was rewarded by a patient look.
'Jonas, it is a wild animal that can now no longer lead its pack, let alone defend itself, and although it was what was in the creature that wanted to hurt you, the beast is now disabled and it would've been a kindness. Nature does not allow for such fragilities and it may be cast out now from his troop and will, in all likelihood suffer a long and

lingering death.'

I absorbed his words with a sense of regret. As much as the baboon had scared and wanted to kill me, I could not help but feel dismay at its plight. I had within me I a deep compassionate love for all animals and could never countenance harming any. But I understood his point and bowed my head in acknowledgement.

'And so how did you do it?' I asked after some moments of eating and it was Samuel's turn to look askance.

'What do you mean?' he said the spoon poised before his mouth.

'The voice in my ear and the best form of attack; is this something you will be able to teach me?'

He looked at me blankly.

'Jonas, I do not know what you are talking about.'

'When the baboon was about to throw the sand in my eyes you told me to use the *Vajra* manoeuvre. Your voice came from right behind me. I heard you as clearly as I hear you now, I swear!'

I stared at his bemused expression and was further perplexed as his face then creased into a delighted grin and he gave out a rich chuckle.

'Why, that wasn't me, boy!'

'Then who...?' and then it dawned on me.

'The angel? Was that the *angel* stood behind me and whose voice I heard!'

I felt a rush of pleasure go through me as the hairs at the back of neck stood up.

'But he sounded just like you! So much so I would've sworn on my life that it *was* you! But, but ... how ...'

'If he had used his own voice, you would not have recognised it and such a distraction could have proved fatal,' my uncle interjected, 'so he used mine instead, knowing there would less chance of you turning and leaving yourself open to the beast.'

He waved a piece of *injera*, 'I am a man of many things, but being able to throw my voice like that would be way beyond my capabilities; an angel, however ...' and he winked.

'So I am being watched over,' I said wonderingly.

'Yes, did you ever doubt it?'

I bent my head down to my meal as this latest development sank in, as did the image of the baboon's fury as it launched itself at me and I

heard once again in my head the deep musical voice that had calmly urged direction that had undoubtedly saved my life.
And in a silent guilty moment of childish regret how I wish that voice had been my fathers.
I thought of all the years I had yearned for some memory of the man whose existence had been as elusive to me as it had been mysterious. Of how my mother's face would still light up when she'd talk about him. His kind, easy manner, his love for his family, his pride in God's work and the fierceness of spirit he unleashed when dealing with the dark side.
Of the latter she spoke little, but enough for me to know that demons were real and that 'bad things' walked the earth and would devour you if you weren't careful.
Having missed death by inches just that very day I knew now that her words were less of a warning and more of a promise, and I determined there and then to make every day of training and preparation count.
And so I did. I worked harder. I listened more keenly. I drank, absorbed, and all but breathed each and every essence of learning that was given to me.
My uncle was an excellent teacher, and by the time we came from the mountains there was a new confidence in my stride and a toughening of spirit.

We were welcomed back with the customary enthusiasm, my mother leading from the front, and that night as the whole village celebrated by firelight, I was approached by the elders.
'Jonas, as you know your names means 'the chosen one', and although you are not an official member of this tribe, you are affiliated nevertheless, by the ancestry of your father and your blood. Therefore as a rite of passage and a mark of your status, we wish to offer you the sign of your caste so you will always carry the mark of your sacred calling.'
I looked to my mother who was listening and she gave an imperceptible nod, and by the time the time sun rose the next morning all pain was forgotten as I tenderly fingered the tattoos on my face.
It had been a painful process, marked by much ceremony as one of

the elder tribesmen pierced the soft skin of my cheeks carefully. The village had looked on silently, and when he'd finished and my face was smoothed with a sweet-smelling balm followed by much singing and celebration.

'Jonas, you have boyhood behind; you are, in the eyes of God and your brethren now known as *Bekele*. May the blessed hand of the Almighty always be upon you.'

My mother gave me a fierce hug.

'Your father would be so proud! You have made *me* proud! You are a true warrior of spirit now, Jonas, and of the *Bekele*. *Ai*! How I will never forget this moment!'

Caught up in the excitement it was some time before I was able to find a quiet moment and seeing Samuel stood back in the shadows I went to him.

'Uncle, this name, *Bekele* what does it mean?'

His eyes were unusually bright from the firelight and they regarded me with just a hint of merriment.

'Why, you need not look so worried, Jonas, it merely means *he who has come into his own,* and so you have!'

'These markings ... they are so that people will know who I am?'

'Not quite, *Bekele*.' he replied tersely all humour gone, 'people will notice them, of course – how could they not? But unlike many of our neighbouring tribes that bear tattoos, yours is not of African extraction. These markings come from a time much older, which is why they have the blue of the *woad* that we grow and have done for centuries. Your tattoo has a significant meaning, but only those who blight this earth with their presence will know.'

'The dark forces, you mean?'

'What else? You now bear the marks that will set you apart and make many think twice before they come at you.'

'Unlike the mountain baboon ...'

Samuel gave me a level look.

'That does not mean you will not come under attack, Jonas, and in ways you least expect – you are their enemy, remember? And a potent one at that! They know your purpose, but the tattoo's are a sign of divine protection and denotes clearly where you're from ...'

'Which is where, uncle?' I chipped in and was rewarded with another

look. 'Am I of Africa or the Holy Land? Forgive me interrupting but from what culture exactly am I from?'
Samuel spread his hand in an all-encompassing gesture.
'Why, from them all, Jonas, from them all ...'
'But how does that answer my question? If anything I am even more confused. What does this mean, uncle, and will I ever learn the truth?'
'Yes, in time, and when he decides it's right.' And with that Samuel pointed heavenwards before strolling off.
The meaning was unmistakable and I would have to be satisfied with that. But then who was I question the *mystique* of an almighty God? I was of a sacred line, whether I liked it or not, and fingering the raised bumps that would now define me, I felt a thrill of pride at my new-found status.
How this facial disfigurement would be greeted back home, however, was a different matter, but in the final days of our visit we put such concerns behind us although my mother did confide that the only person she was worried about was my stepfather.
'Once he's over the shock, I don't doubt he will understand our reasoning - we are from different cultures after all, and he is nothing if not a man of the world. But there be worse reactions in other areas, your school especially, but we will face them together. You are a son to be proud of, Jonas, and I will not deny you your birthright and the rites of your passage!'
'I will say that it was my idea. That I wanted to bear the marks of my father and that you didn't know...' I began and she shook her head vigorously.
'No. I will not have you lie; we will deal with this together. Rhys deserves nothing less than the truth and I would not seek to deceive him. I consider myself blessed to be given the love of a good man once more, and so with this in mind, know that my past and my present must end here.'
'What do you mean?'
There was something in her words that filled me with an uncanny sense of sorrow and taking my hands in hers she fixed me with her beautiful eyes.
'What I'm saying, Jonas, is that I will not be coming back. My life is with our new family in Wales and so I must shake the dust from my

beloved Africa and leave the ghost of your father behind.'

At my stricken look she squeezed my hands tightly.

'Do not look so sad, Jonas. He will reside in my heart forever, and never will I forget the great love between us and the best gift he could have ever given me, which is you,' she loosened her hold and smiling gently added, 'We are all part of a greater plan and until we meet again our paths must differ. Life will go on and whatever waits for us both in the future; know that between us we have given you the best chance there is. I bid you have peace in your heart, Jonas, for you will return – indeed you are now just beginning your journey. And so let not the echoes of yesteryear divert you from *your* path. Your time is nearly upon you, and God will show you the way.'

A shout from outside broke the moment and she dropped my hands.

'They are waiting to honour us with a farewell feast and so I will not have you sit at their table with a long face. You are nearly a man, Jonas, and when we leave here you will leave the boy behind and I, my past life. So, come, let us go celebrate, for Lord knows there will be attention of a different kind when we get home!'

Chapter 6

She was not wrong; but then my mother rarely was. My stepfather's shouts all but raised the dead when he first saw my face, but he waited until we were in the parking area of the airport before he let fly. Thankfully my siblings had been left with a neighbour because I had never seen him so angry.

Heads turned and then quickly looked away as he vented his fury, his strong accent accentuated by his ire and with a blasphemy thrown in here and there for good measure. My mother waited serenely until he had finished.

'They are sacred markings, Rhys,' she said soothingly, 'worn only by his father's kin. It is part of his heritage and will give him the spiritual protection he needs. It has been a shock, I know, but as you yourself have often said, God works in mysterious ways, and whether we like it or not, these markings are a sign of *His* favour, and have been so since he sent such as my son into the world.'

My father had looked at her exasperated but he could not argue with that and she knew it!

'I have missed you, *cariad*. Please do not be angry with me ...' she murmured in the knowledge that the storm was now passing and I saw my stepfather's features soften but he wasn't quite done yet.

'*Iesu Grist* you could charm the birds from the trees, woman! But you are forgetting about his school, not to mention the rest of the village once they clap eyes on him! We'll be lucky if we're not reported to Social Services!'

My mother looked aghast at that.

'You cannot ... you do not think ...'

'Who knows!' said my stepfather grimly, 'But no doubt we'll soon find out!'

He then turned his attention to me as I stood by quietly and in a softer voice said, 'Well, it looks as though tattoos on your face aren't the only surprise you've brought back from Africa, Jonas. You've grown at least another two feet!'

He was exaggerating of course although admittedly I had gained an extra inch or so, but it was a sign that his anger was abating and after giving me a firm hug he enquired whether the raised bumps on my face were sore.

'No, not so much now and I'm healing really well,' I replied with just a touch of eagerness. It disturbed me to see this man so distressed for he had never been anything but a kindly figure to me, 'I'm sorry I've upset you, I ...'

He raised a hand.

'There is no need, Jonas, let us leave it there. But I think we are going to be in for a rocky few days, just as long as you both know that. There will be no sweet-talking the authorities, Abeba, should they want to get involved!'

By this time my mother had recovered her composure.

'Then let them get involved for no one is more involved than God himself and it is in *him* I trust.'

Once again she silenced her husband with her strength of her argument and by the time we set off for the long drive home, peace had been restored and I felt my eyes closing. Lulled by the murmur of their voices my last thought before I drifted into sleep was whether my real father ever looked over me and then I slept.

A heavy rain was falling by the time we pulled into our village, and as we drew up in front of the cottage my siblings, who had spotted us from the neighbours house and came running. Their exuberance at having their mother and older brother back home was evident as they jumped all around us in between hugs and excited questions, but it was the facial tattoos on my face that drew the most attention and it gave all of us some insight as to what to expect.

'Can we do this in the house?' Rhys grumbled, 'We're all getting soaked to the skin!' He waved to Mrs Parry the neighbour who'd stuck her head out and thanked her for minding the children. I saw her eyes widen as she saw my face with the knowledge she'd be knocking on the door before the hour was out.

We'd brought presents, of course, just simple handmade gifts that caused much delight, but the attention kept coming back to me and seeing my growing discomfort Rhys suggested we go for a walk. I didn't need asking twice, and besides it would probably be best that I wasn't in the house when Mrs Parry came a-calling. My mother was more than capable of dealing with curious people, she'd had years of it and had become quite adept.

'The rain has practically stopped and even the sun's trying to come out; not that it'll be as hot as you've had it in Africa.' he said pulling on a light anorak, 'You've missed a typical Welsh summer, Jonas! We won't be long, love.'

He dropped a kiss onto my mother's head and then we were out of the back door and soon on the track that led up to the mountains.

The cool moist air was like a gentle caress on my face and I breathed deeply as my stepfather cast me glances that were a mixture of worry and bemusement before finally asking, 'So how was it?'

As we wound our way up through the wet grass I told him everything, except about the vision of the angel. He gasped and then whistled when he heard about my encounter with the mountain baboon and showed great interest in the principles of my new fighting skills.

'*Kalari,*' he mused, 'I've never heard of it, I'll look forward to you demonstrating some moves. But it is this strange staff that I'm looking forward to seeing most of all; although I think it best you keep it out of reach of your brother and sister. Just to be sure ...'

We'd reached the top of the ridge and stopped as we always did to look out across the vale. In my mind's eye I could still see the lush sweep of the valleys amidst the splendour of the Simien mountains; but there were no wild creatures that would attack you here, and as the clouds scudded across the pale skies I knew in my heart that it was possible to love two places.

'You are nearly sixteen, Jonas and considered a man back in that other continent, but here, as you know, it's much different. Yet I feel you are about to embark on something that is beyond both of our control, and if I am to be honest, I don't mind telling you that it scares me a bit.'

I looked down into that rugged well-loved face and frowned.

'You - *scared*? The ex-bare knuckle-champ of the South Wales Valleys! No, dad, I don't believe it! Why, what's changed?'

'You, son, you ...' He replied fixing me with his blue-eyed stare and for the first time since I'd known this remarkable man I saw uncertainty and not a little fear..

'But Dad, I'm still me, I'm still, Jonas, I ...'
'Son,' he interjected, 'you've had a three week stint up in the mountains of another country in the company of your blood-kin, fought off a wild beast not once but *twice!* Have learned an ancient art of combat and how to be a man! Oh, and your mother tells me you've also become a vegetarian! What's that all about? So much change, Jonas, so change and life will never be the same again. Life - within this community, will never be the same again! And I fear for your safety now because you stand out more than you *ever* have.'
He laid a hand on my arm and gazed at me earnestly.
'We have discussed many times your desire to take up the cloth and dedicate your life to the service of God. Tell me, Jonas; is this what you want to do or has this changed?'
I felt his love wash over me as I did his concern and placing my hand over his said, 'No, dad, not at all. If anything I feel the need to shut myself away and study even more, for there are things my uncle told me that cannot be unlearned, or discovered in an ordinary place of learning ...'
I deliberately left the sentence unfinished and his face crumpled with relief.
'Then thank God for that, because when I saw you at the airport with your face ... your face ...' there was raw emotion in his voice that surprised me but I waited for him to find the words.
'At first I thought you would be telling me you wanted to return home and start a new life with your people.'
I smiled widely at that and gave him a playful punch on the arm.
'Now why would I want to do that! This is my home; this is where I grew up, isn't it? And this is where I'll stay ... but that's not saying I won't go back.'
He nodded, 'And your mother?'
'I'm afraid you're going to be stuck with her!' and we both burst out laughing for because whatever was in the future, we knew we would face it together, and as we made our way back down we sang an old Welsh hymn as the sheep watched us pass with their usual curiosity.

I had a few days until school term resumed and spent much of it recovering from the jet-lag. The inclement weather made it easier to stay indoors as it would seem that summer was well and truly over, and I buried my head in my books whenever my siblings would allow me.

The tattoos on my face continued to fascinate them and they would pester me continually wanting to touch the raised markings asking for the hundredth time if it hurt.

My mother had tried to prevail upon the goodwill of Mrs Parry to remain discreet, but such an unprecedented event simply couldn't be borne and by the time I returned to school, the word was practically out.

My father accompanied me on that first morning, and as his glares met the shocked and whispering faces I was reminded of how he had often done the same when I was a small child. Only now I towered above him and we made, I knew, a strange sight as walked through the streets.

Not least because I felt like Goliath walking beside David, united in our fight against a common enemy, which in this case, of course would be the school authorities – and that was just for starters!

As we went into reception Rhys bid me to stay outside as he tapped the door before stepping into the main office. The school secretary looked affronted at this intrusion and rose from behind her desk.

'You can't just walk in! What ...'

'I would like to see the headmaster, please.'

There was an authority in my stepfather's voice that brooked no argument, but the secretary accustomed to getting her own way drew herself up haughtily.

'Unless you've made an appointment then I'm afraid that's impossible. It's the first day of term, Mr Llewellyn and the headmaster is extremely busy ...' she paused with just a hint of smugness adding, 'Most ... *people* call to make an appointment. Perhaps you'd like to give me a ring later and I'll see what I can do.'

As a heavy silence fell between them I could imagine my stepfather's face. It was a thinly-veiled slight and he wasn't the kind of man to take it lightly.

Despite his instruction to stay outside I stepped into the office and the effect was instant.

With an audible gasp the secretary's mouth dropped open and she

scuttled into the back calling, *'Mr Davies? Mr Davies?'*
When she re-emerged with the headmaster in tow she hovered feverishly in the background like some insect caught in a jar as we waited for the storm to break.
'Dear God!' breathed Mr Davies and stood stock-still for some moments staring at me in horror. 'What on *earth* have you done?'
'What God has done, you mean!' quipped Rhys.
'What?' the headmaster gaped briefly at him before dragging his eyes back to my face.
'No matter,' said Rhys smartly, 'As you are probably aware Jonas has spent most of the summer with his family back in Ethiopia, and as part of his culture ...'
'Culture!' Mr Davies echoed as though half-asleep.
'Yes, his culture, Mr Davies, and as you know they do things differently there and so to mark the occasion of Jonas's coming of age, he was offered the tribal tattoo and, as you can see, he accepted!'
'*He* ... accepted? What...where was his mother?'
The headmaster was obviously recovering his wits as his mind absorbed the enormity of the situation.
'His mother was present and she agreed,' replied Rhys with his customary boldness. 'But ultimately it was Jonas's choice. Nobody forced him into it. I just want you to be clear about that.'
'Clear about *what?* The boy's face will never be clear of these ... these markings for the rest of his life! What on earth were you thinking, Jonas? And more to the point, what was his *mother!*'
His countenance took on something of a set look as he visibly drew himself together.
'You know I'm going to have to report this. This is on a par with child abuse and ...'
'Don't you dare! Don't you dare even *go there!*' barked my stepfather in his best pulpit voice and Mr Davies shrank back.
'Rhys, look ...'
'Rhys look nothing! It is a custom of his people! It is something he wanted to bring back from his culture, *his culture,* do you understand? And as Welsh as you or I or anyone else *thinks* he should be, his bloodline is from *Africa!* His *colour* is from *Africa!* And if he wanted to embrace that part of his heritage with a face-full of tattoos'

then let that be the case and let's have no more allegations of child abuse because I will not have it, I'm telling you! *Iesu Grist!'*
Mr Davies found his voice after some moments and held out his hands in a placating gesture.
'Alright, alright, wrong term perhaps, but I'm not so sure Social Services will agree, and you have to admit, Rhys, it isn't everyday you see *anyone,* never mind one of my pupils, walking round with a face-full of tattoos, and I'm afraid I'm going to have to tell you now,' and he cast me an apologetic look, 'I cannot have Jonas back in the school looking like that.'
'Why not?' asked my stepfather in a tight voice.
The headmaster spread his hands further.
'Why do you think! Surely I do not have to spell it out?'
He turned to look up at me and took in my face. I sensed a deep distaste amidst the disbelief but I met his gaze squarely.
'I am sorry, Jonas, but ...' he shook his head as though unable to find the words and then returning to my father he added, 'It's a shame, because he's a bright boy, indeed academically he was one of our best students and it ...'
'Leave it there, if you please,' interrupted my father, 'you speak of him as though he is not in the room and I'm not having that. Make your phone calls, cast your aspersions, but know ... *know* ... that I will fight *all* of you *all* the way if you so much as try to bring a charge of child abuse against me or my wife, and that I will call on the court of Human Rights if I have to!'
As the Mr Davies positively wilted before him the school secretary moaned softly as she stood riveted next to her desk, and I could almost feel sorry for them. My stepfather was a force to be reckoned with once he got his dander up and his impassioned energy combined with a fighting past made him a formidable opponent.
Without further ado, he turned smartly on his heel saying, 'Come along Jonas, let's leave them to it! I'll not have you where you're not wanted. God takes care of his own and we'll finish your education somewhere else. - even if I have to pay for a tutor myself!'
With this parting shot he stalked from the building and I felt like Moses when we walked across the playground. Bodies parted collectively like the Red Sea as jaws dropped and mouths fell open.

But I kept my eyes ahead as my stepfather strode purposely forward and led the way out of the gates. The silence we left in our wake was uncanny until the school bell sounded and it seemed to break the spell as voices came to life in an excitable babble and I knew in that moment that nothing would ever be the same again and that such attention would be a constant companion for the rest of my life.

Chapter 7

My old headmaster had obviously wasted no time for within the hour we had all manner of local authorities knocking at the door, and in anticipation of this my stepfather had contacted the local bishop and other high-ranking officials of the church and soon our cottage became the hub of unparalleled activity as a small crowd gathered outside.

The police were in attendance, of course, in case it was decided I should be taken into care, but after satisfying themselves that I was in no apparent danger, and faced with the united front of the church, everyone finally calmed down and proceeded in a more informal manner.

I was taken into the parlour and interviewed at length, my stepfather bristling beside me.

'Were you pressured into having these tattoos, Jonas?'

' Did you feel as though you couldn't say no at the time?'

'Why did you feel the need to do this to yourself?'

I couldn't tell them the real reason of course, they would never understand, and as I answered each question in a calm quiet voice, they finally ran out of questions and looked askance at each other not really sure what to do next.

'We will have to file a report, of course, and just so you're aware we will be making further visits just to ascertain that Jonas's education will be continuing. Have you a proposal in mind for this, Mr Llewellyn?'

The senior social worker glanced nervously at my stepfather. His past occupation and involvement with the church was legendary in our area and he commanded a lot of respect. He was the kind of man who would make *tsunami's* not waves and everyone who knew him knew it.

'My diocese have agreed to assist and will take on my son's education and will arrange for a tutor.' He emphasized the word *son* in such a way it was all but a challenge, 'Then it will be up to Jonas what it is he will want to do then – although he has expressed an interest in taking vows and going into the church.'

Their eyebrows shot up at that and I had an overwhelming urge to laugh, because I knew that this information had startled them as much as it rendered them speechless, and in that instant I also knew that everything would blow over and there would be no charges brought. The fact there was such strong representation from the church sat just in the next room made it all the more difficult and even our local *Heddlu* were shuffling about looking ill at ease.

Once it had been established that there was no further 'risk to my well-being', it was with no small relief for everyone when this awkward and impromptu gathering to an end.

My mother, after being interviewed and disapprovingly taken to task, was as serene as ever and had been busy providing refreshments with the help of Mrs Parry. It would've been easier to have kept a wildfire out than our neighbour who was agog at these developments and inwardly saving every little snippet her eyes busy behind her glasses. Even in such an unusual situation Welsh hospitality was unstinting and it was played out regardless as officials came and officials went reports were made and assurances given. Most of the people present all knew each other which allowed for a certain lack of formality, and by the time the last government body had, left all questions that could possibly be asked had been voiced, logged and answered.

The only person who remained behind was the bishop for he wanted to speak to my stepfather privately, and after they had sequestered in the back parlour for some time they called me in.

The bishop was a plump, kindly man who was only one of the very few people who was aware of my calling. The fact he accommodated what many would regard as *hocus-pocus,* or even blasphemy, was an indication of how highly he held my father in regard.

The fact they had also grown up together helped tremendously in having ecclesiastical powers of the church on-side, and now he wanted to talk to me about what my options were for the future since matters had now been brought forward.

'Once your schooling is complete we will have to think how best to proceed with your vocation to enter the ministry, and in view of your youth, never mind your ... er ... appearance, influence will need to be brought to bear at the highest level. You must understand that you are going to be under the most rigorous scrutiny once word of your special standing become apparent,' he paused and gave me a meaningful look, 'I hope you realise that you're also going to have to go away in order for the church to facilitate the uniqueness of your abilities, Jonas, that you will not be able to stay here. You will be able to visit, yes, but for as long as you will be required to study, such intense training will have to be undertaken elsewhere. Do you understand what it is I'm saying?'

I glanced at my stepfather in surprise and he gave a small nod.

My heart dropped with a slow sinking feeling. I loved my family and had assumed I would be training down in Llandaff which meant I could commute the journey between Cardiff and home quite easily. The phone rang in the hall as it had been doing for the umpteenth time, for already the local press had got hold of the story, and it was obvious to me then why I couldn't stay and I bowed my head in assent.

'It won't be so bad, Jonas,' said Rhys, 'Lord knows it could have been a lot worse had you been taken into care! We will come up and see you often, and as Bishop Evans says, you'll still be able to visit.' He gave me a crooked grin, 'I'll miss our walks, but you'll be in good hands and it won't be for a few days yet, until things are put in place, isn't that right, Barry?'

The bishop nodded and didn't seem to mind my stepfather's familiarity but then their history was a long one.

'So where will I go? You mentioned 'up'?' My gaze was on Rhys and he looked away.

'Bangor.' replied the bishop,

'Bangor? But that's *miles* away!'

'It's near enough, and with recent events, you haven't really left us much choice, I'm afraid, Jonas. They'd sniff you out in St. David's, and Llandaff obviously is out of the question, but North Wales will be far enough away to deter the keenest reporter and besides, it is my belief you'll like it. It's not a big place, but it is an area steeped in religious history and surrounded by the most beautiful scenery. It will be the perfect!'

'And it's not half as far away as Africa,' added Rhys, 'although they do have mountains!'

It was his attempt at humour, I knew and I offered a weak smile.
Bangor!
'Right, then I'd best be off and get arrangements underway. It would probably be wise to stay in the house until it's time for us to collect you,' the bishop said rising to his feet. I stood respectfully and he gazed up at me with an unreadable expression on his face.
'My word, but God broke the mold when he made you didn't he, Jonas ...'
And as I stood before him uncertainly he surprised me with a pat on the shoulder before saying, 'God bless you, my son, we will take care of you and in every way. You are under our protection now, so don't worry.'
Then turning to my stepfather, he said briskly, 'Rhys, be so kind as to thank your lady-wife for the tea and her forbearance during what has been a challenging few hours for us all, and fear not, we will deal with any further enquiries from the authorities.' He glanced at his watch before pulling on his coat and we walked him to the door. The small crowd outside had dispersed and a low mist had descended adding a distinct chill to the air. It fitted my mood perfectly.

I had heard stories that the people of North Wales had no love for their Southern cousins – throw in the fact I was obviously not of natural Welsh extraction and I was anticipating no particular welcome in their hillsides! It was a discomforting thought, as was the realisation that for the first time in my life I would be far away from my family and utterly alone. It was a daunting prospect indeed. So no one was surprised more than me when within just a couple of weeks of moving in I found I actually liked it!
Bangor was the size of a small town but officially a city and the Welsh language the principle tongue. Overlooked by the mountains of Snowdonia on one side, they in turn looked out across the Menai Strait to the last stronghold of the Druids, *Ynys Mon* – the Isle of Anglesey, where once lay the palaces of Welsh Princes amidst fields of golden corn.
I was very taken with the cathedral and quickly became interested in all aspects of the secular, as well as the religious features in the area. History was rich in this part of Wales and with my ever-open mind I

absorbed everything that came my way and gladly, for here was so different to what I was used to in the Valleys, and yet in some ways almost the same, and it wasn't long before my rudimentary command of the Welsh language became fully fluent.

Generally I was made to feel very welcome although my face elicited that initial shock, as did my height for I seemed to tower over everybody – even my main tutor, Einion, who was six foot one.

This meant that I was stared at, of course, but in a more covert way, but I became less bothered by the looks and submerged myself into my studies with a ready acceptance as books, doctrines and scriptures took over.

My family visited as often as they could and would exclaim excitedly at how much I'd grown.

'Life seems to be treating you well, I have to say!' my stepfather would enthuse, 'Already within six months you have left the gangling boy back in the valleys and are fast drawing on the mantle of a man, not to mention a few more inches everytime we see you!' He tipped me a wink, 'Are you sure you won't reconsider a career in the ring, Jonas?'

'My word, what are they feeding you? Your ankles are showing beneath your trousers! Rhys, he can't walk around like that, we'll have to go to town!'

As always my mother would find something that needed changing, tweaking, adjusting.

'You are still my son,' she would say in answer to my protests, 'and there are some things only a mother can see!'

That they were proud of me, I knew, and visibly relieved when informed I had been awarded a discretionary scholarship for the remainder of my studies. Money was tight for many living in the South Wales valleys, even for those in employment, and my family was no exception. The trip to Ethiopia had taken much of their savings and I was determined not to be a burden financially or otherwise.

The Diocese also gave me a small allowance which allowed for small treats and trips out. It wasn't much but then my needs were small and I rewarded their kindness by working hard.

Within the year I had sat and passed all exams required of me before moving on to more intense and spiritual study and during this time I also made my first real friends.

Their names were Steffan and Menna and they were non-identical twins.
In between classes I was keen to discover more about the local area and was particularly taken with the Island of Anglesey. Despite the usual stares and speculation I would hop on a bus at any given opportunity and go off and explore. Steffan and Menna were both students at the local University and for some inexplicable reason our paths would cross often to the point we had become on nodding terms. One day, as I stood waiting at the bus stop they pulled up in a light-coloured fiesta that had seen better days.
'Off on a jaunt again?' called Menna through the window. She was a striking-looking girl with tawny eyes and a beautiful mane of copper-coloured hair, but even without the good looks there was an attractive vitality about her. She beamed at me now as her brother craned his head behind her grinning.
He shared the same tawny looks but his features were more square and his complexion paler. I smiled back, albeit a bit shyly.
'Give you a lift?' he said, 'we thought we'd go to Penmon if you fancy joining us?'
My heart lifted. I'd heard of Penmon, of course and had always wanted to visit, but it was at the far east of the island and you needed a car to reach it.
I didn't need asking twice, and soon there was much hilarity as I squeezed myself into the back of the car, but it was all good-natured and soon I was laughing with them.
'Try not to dent the roof!' cried Steffan in mock concern.
'I told you we needed a soft-top, Steffan!' added Menna as we all dissolved into giggles, and somehow I managed to semi-slouch into a position with the seatbelt around me.
The drama of me getting in had well and truly broke any remaining ice and soon we were all chatting like long-lost friends as the little car crossed the Britannia bridge that spanned the Strait.
It turned out they were two years older than me. But what really struck me about them both was that they seemed genuinely interested

in *me* as a person, not just in my appearance. They were also keen to impart news about themselves; Steffan was studying History and Archaeology, Menna, Philosophy and Religious Studies, the latter of which was not lost on me.

'You're always going to the Island,' remarked Menna, 'what's there?' I shrugged.

'I'm not really sure – the place draws me and there's just so much history. Take the Romans, for instance, and how their invasion of this island very nearly didn't happen once they clapped eyes on the inhabitants! Apparently the sight of them instilled such terror the commanders had to threaten all sorts to get them to cross the strait. '

'Ah, the purge, or should one say the massacre of the Druids!' said Steffan and shook his head sadly, 'They finally crossed alright, and despite the best efforts of the defenders – men and women alike - the Romans killed the lot of them. They also set fire to their sacred groves so that nothing would be left to even say they were there ... but then they were pagans after all and into human sacrifice, if reports are to be believed.'

'You're not going over there hunting for old ghosts are you, Jonas?' And it was only when I saw the twinkle in the hazel eyes that I realised Menna was joking.

'Well if you love ancient history, then you'll love Penmon. It truly is a special place. Our parents used to bring us here for picnics in the school holidays.'

The twins were from a small market town called Bala, and having found the people of North Wales to be more reserved than their southerly counterparts, the open friendliness of this duo came as something to a surprise. The fact they wanted be friends with *me*, markings and all, indicated a warm and loving spirit, and I was deeply touched by their acceptance of the fact I was so different.

'So what's with the tattoos, then, and why are they a blue colour?' The question was inevitable but I was still struck by Menna's no-nonsense approach before being amused in turn by Steffan's indignant one.

'*Menna!* You can't blurt it out like that!' He flicked me an apologetic glance in the mirror but before I could answer his sister chipped back in.

'Well, it looks like I just have, Steffan! You don't mind, do you, Jonas? I bet you get asked that question all the time!' she craned round and peeped at me through a tangle of bronzed hair and catching a mischievous glint I smiled.

'No, I don't mind at all. People usually just stare but I rarely get asked. So in answer to your question, it's just a tribal marking from my kin back in Ethiopia and the indigo dye is just something they use.'

I kept my tone light – I couldn't tell them the truth, of course.

Steffan gave a snort.

'I could have told you that, Menna! Talk about putting poor old Jonas on the spot. Apologies, my friend, but my sister can at times be a law unto herself!'

'Which is why I was the first born between us because somebody had to take control,' Menna turned again and winked at me as her brother huffed good-naturedly.

I found I was enjoying their company immensely. Just to be able to banter and behave as young people my age did made for a refreshing change. I was quite solemn for my years, I knew, and came across as being older than I was.

Little did I know then that their simple offer of a lift that day would set in motion a whole series of events that would test my faith and break my heart – and I often wondered in the years that followed if their coming into my life at that time was all part of a bigger picture that God had deliberately designed or if I could have done things differently.

But these thoughts were in the future and as we passed through Beaumaris and came finally to the sacred site of Penmon the twins suddenly fell silent.

A fine mist had come in from the sea and was shrouding the grey buildings as though trying to hide them from sight. I sensed a shifting in the air, even from within the confines of the car, and seemingly the twins did too. We gazed out until Steffan eventually said,

'You go on ahead, Jonas. We'll stay here for a minute or two. It's always good to get a feel of this place on your own, and besides, we've been here many times ...'

Menna turned her head and gave a nod, and I was grateful for their sensitivity. Something was afoot, I could feel it in the air, and they, on some inexplicable level, sensed it too.

I nodded and carefully extricated myself from the car, my eyes searching the mist as the sun valiantly tried to reassert itself through the haze. The sudden change in the weather was quite uncanny but was an odd energy about the place that seemed to draw me.

I didn't so much as glance at the other buildings, but I was aware of a church and what looked like a dovecote as whatever was pulling me drew me further into the site towards a rocky outcrop where tucked on the end was a crudely-built hut.

I stopped and stared towards the strange dwelling as the hair began to prickle along the back of my neck.

Something or *someone* was waiting inside for me. Something so old, so ancient, that I had no name or concept of who, or what it could be. I stilled my breathing and my heartbeat slowed as my inner eye tried to penetrate the weathered facade. But I could feel nothing and I needed to know before I went any further,

And then I heard it, in the softest voice.

Dewch chi mewn.

Chapter 8.

For a moment I thought my mind was playing tricks and I frowned before the words came again.
Come in...
I was being invited to enter. But to what? And more importantly - *by what!*
The mist swirled around me like a living thing as though trying to pull me forward.
I reached out with a force of my own not unlike when a fisherman casts his net, and this time I had a result.
I felt my eyes widen in disbelief and a ripple passed through me like a warm wind.
I took one step, then another, and as soon as I dipped my head and stepped into the tiny space I immediately knew why I had been drawn to this place - and judging by the smile on the face of the figure before me - he had been expecting me.
'Croeso, dyn sanctaidd ... and so finally you have come.'
Of all the experiences I'd had up to that moment there were several things about this one that struck me all at once, but I could say nothing for some moments as I took in the small figure sat calmly across from me on the stone bench. Even the birds seemed to stop singing as the man called Saint Seriol, son of a King and founder of Penmon, regarded me with eyes of the palest blue that looked out from a face that was even paler. A luxuriant beard as white as snow forked in the middle and almost as long as the braided hair. Around his person he wore a simple robe of no particular colour and his whole being seemed to pulsate gently as though energised by an unseen force.
St. Seriol the Fair!
It was an incredible moment as it was unexpected. I had read about him and of his counterpart, St. Cybi, of course, but what did this mean, and why was he here?.
'Do not be afraid. I am as you see me, and I am here in the light of all that's good. Come closer.'

His voice was low and melodious with a natural command that held a distinct but long-lost accent. It seemed to float across the very air as the pale eyes held me fast. We regarded each other silently for some moments and I was aware that he was looking not just at me, but *into* me, as you would a mystery.

I waited my head slightly bowed in profound respect for he had addressed me as 'holy man', but in the face of his spiritual presence I suddenly felt all of my seventeen years and would have knelt if the enclosed space would have allowed it.

'Ah, I see your mind and there is no need for you to kneel before me, Jonas.'

He knew my name!

'You are of a spirit caste that is older than mine, and so I meet with you now as an equal, for there are things you must know and from my lips only. Time is short so mark me well, for I would speak to you of what you are and things to come, for you will encounter those of the highest standing and they will test you much and without mercy, and so I will aid you in your quest ...' and with that he began to speak in an archaic language that was not like any Welsh I had ever heard before, and yet to my amazement I understood every word of it as the hairs rose slowly on the back of my neck.

I listened intently and with a growing apprehension, for these were not glad tidings sent to gird an innocent heart. These were strange words, dark words, imbued with deep and meaningful warning, and a revelation of such spiritual magnitude it shocked me to the core.

At this final disclosure I drew back visibly shaken.

His response was to smile enigmatically, the light-coloured eyes still holding me fast.

'You seem unsure ... as though perhaps you are not certain, and yet you have more right than many.'

I regarded him in silence for some moments before finding my tongue.

'It is quite incredible. I had always thought of myself from one of the Lost Tribes, descended from a man who was reviled in his time, and who made a new start under the guise of a whole different people. This is what I have been told, and yet – this, *this!'* I shook my head in wonder. 'But it explains why my father's people are different and has never followed the Semitic creed. Why they would not repatriate to Israel when the chance presented itself, last but not least, why the tribe have always held themselves aloof – even from Ethiopian identity because they ... we ... are from neither of these places and never have been!'

'So now you understand. Now clearly do you see. For you are from this land, this place, and your bloodline began here, in this very country when all was one and God known by another name. So let there be no doubt surrounding the question of your heritage anymore, Jonas! Your line goes back to the beginnings of time before man ventured forth and traversed new continents. Know also that one day this knowledge shall be made known to all and that none may refute it for the evidence will be right before their eyes by way of their science.'

I let the words sink in. It was an incredible revelation, an unprecedented development that the elders of the tribe had hinted at and held back from me.

'There will be those who will not like it,' I ventured, 'indeed it is my opinion there will be many who will oppose it – such is the common belief that the first men of this country were of white skin not black. They will not like it.'

The aura that surrounded the saint appeared to flare and a darkness stole into the pale stare for a moment.

'It matters not what they like, as it matters not what they believe! The proof shall be in their findings and these will prevail in the face of all argument. A sacred tribe once walked this land and you are one of the few descendents that are able to harness the old ways.'

My mind went to my inner eye, the uncanny fighting skills, and the ability to pick up new languages easily, and then of course there was the ability to see, hear and commune with spirits. A sudden thought occurred to me.

'But what about the bible, the teachings, the scriptures? How does all of this fit in?'

The figure before me shifted and came closer, favouring me with an indecipherable look.

'There are many things that have been written in the name of God, but how much was God-given and how much written by the hand of

man..? Aye, I see your shock, as well, I speak the truth. You just need to find it for yourself, and so I bid you, look and keep looking, search and keep searching, for the day will come soon enough when you will have need of the answers – but not just for yourself...'

It was an extraordinary statement and a disturbing if not blasphemous one at that, and I truly did not know what to say.

'You bear the sacred markings. You are what you are. Have no fear of the truth and let the old ways guide you ... until then, beware the softness of your heart and keep your spirit open.'

And with that he was gone.

I blinked before shaking my head.

Did that just happen? Did I just really have a conversation with a fifteen hundred year old saint and in an archaic Welsh tongue that I'd never spoken before!

I shook my head some more and rubbed my temples. It was as though I was emerging from a trance but I could still hear his words like a deeply ensconced echo.

And what did he mean by the words *beware the softness of your heart* ... it was obviously meant as a warning, but why?

Suddenly there were voices on the path and I gathered myself quickly. There would be time enough for reflection later. I needed to get back to the twins. They were probably wondering where I was, and although I'd probably only been gone a few minutes it already felt like hours.

The voices had reached the doorway and fell silent at the sight of me. I turned smoothly careful to keep my head from the low ceiling and stepped out into bright sunlight.

The mist had completely disappeared.

Four elderly ladies stood rooted to the spot as they gazed up at me with barely-suppressed horror as I looked about me puzzled. Had I been inside longer than I thought?

The stares finally penetrated and I gave the silent audience a polite nod. There was no return gesture and I was used to that, but I did catch the collective look of distaste just as I turned away, and recalling the revelation of St. Seriol I couldn't help but think, *If only you knew!*

I found the twins sat just beyond the old dovecote enjoying the view across to Puffin Island. I lowered myself down next to them feeling quite surreal and they greeted me casually.
So I could not have been gone that long then, although it seemed like an age. I commented on the view careful to keep my tone light, as though meeting with the shade of a centuries-old saint was something that happened every day. But inwardly my mind was buzzing like a hornet's nest, and I would've given anything to have had a few more minutes in which to settle myself. There must have been something in my voice because Menna turned and looked at me curiously.
'Are you alright, Jonas?'
'Yes, I'm fine.' The lie came readily to my lips and I swallowed it down hastily with no small feeling of shame. But I could hardly blurt out the truth!
'How did you like the holy well? We've seen it dozens of times and so thought we'd leave you to it. And did you see the old ruins next to it? Legend has it that it was where St.Seriol used to live before he moved to the Island.'
She was still staring at me and I took a deep breath. *Get a grip, Jonas!*
'Yes, it was interesting, most ... atmospheric.'
'Well, it's very old, isn't it? I can't imagine how many people must have visited this spot over the centuries with their offerings and prayers.'
'Oh thousands, if not tens of thousands,' proffered Steffan, 'people would come from all over to visit places like this, especially if they thought the waters could affect a cure.'
'And did they?' I said, grateful for the distraction.
Steffan shifted position and squinted at me through the sunlight,
'You're the trainee church-man, Jonas. What do you think?'
I looked out across the small strait to *Ynys Seriol* otherwise known as Puffin Island, the final bastion of a Prince who gave up his privileged position to become a Saint, and my heart swelled with an emotion I could not fathom. For not only he had showed himself to me, but he had passed on the most incredible information and in a tongue lost for all time to the ears of men.
It had been a remarkable experience but I knew I could not share it.

'I cannot think that anywhere this special ... this naturally beautiful, would not be fully blessed by the hand of God,' I said quietly, 'for I have never been in such surroundings than in which I find myself now, and so in answer to your question, my reply would be an unequivocal yes.'

'Why, you are quite the poet, Jonas!' Menna laughed, 'It is also said that Seriol was as much a mystic as a man of God, and so what do you make of that?'

She was watching me closely and I knew that *she knew something*, but before I could rally a reply Steffan gave her playful poke in the ribs.

'Hey, sis, don't start getting all hocus-pocus on us now! Ignore her, Jonas, she gets like this sometimes, reads too many fantasy books when she should be concentrating on her studies. Come on; let's show you the rest of the place, you haven't seen the Dovecote yet!'

As we made our way across to the old cylindrical building I could feel Menna's eyes on me but I kept mine averted as Steffan got into his stride and gave me the full tour. He was knowledgeable and interesting and I found myself relaxing and enjoying the rest of the visit. By the time we returned to the car the sky had clouded over and a light rain was falling.

I paused by the open car door.

'I still don't get it.'

'Don't get what?' echoed Steffan giving me a bemused look.

I lifted my shoulders and glanced up at the sky.

'The weather in this place and how quickly it changes. First we had that mist, then it was sunny, and now it's practically pouring down! How can that be?'

Menna fixed me with a mischievous look before ducking into the car.

'This place is magical ... I *did* try to tell you! Come on, I know it's hard tearing yourself away but you'll get soaked! We'll let you know the next time we come back here, I promise.'

'Thanks, no doubt I'll take you up on your offer, but in the meantime I've enjoyed my visit so much the least I can do is buy you both a bag of chips on the way back to say thank you!'

'Well I won't say no to that!' declared Steffan starting the engine, 'and seriously, it is as Menna says, anytime you feel you want to

come and feel the magic that is Penmon, just say.'
And so began our friendship that saw us scour all the many delights, hidden or otherwise along the North Wales coast, and although we went back to Penmon several times I never saw the old saint again. But I would be aware of Menna watching me closely everytime we walked the site, and although she never openly indicated she sensed something different about me, I respected her sensitivity on this as I did her digression.
This unspoken understanding made for an unusual friendship, and it wasn't long before I found I liked her. I liked her a lot

The next year flew past and amidst the endless study and enjoyment of my new-found friends, my esoteric education was quietly fast-tracked via private lessons and by the time I was eighteen I'd absorbed the equivalent of four years of knowledge in just two and was restless to move on.
I also wanted to return to Africa and see my uncle, for although we kept in touch with the occasional letter I was keen to meet with him and share my encounter with Penmon's Holy Man.
'Patience, Jonas, patience,' Einion my tutor would say as he'd see me gazing out of the window, my eyes faraway, 'There'll be time enough for that, now turn your attention to this passage, please, for it deals specifically with ...' and so I'd bow my head back down to my books as the blaze of an African sun died before me and by the time the Summer holidays came round I had made up my mind.
'Africa! Are you sure?'
The bishop scratched his chin and then looked to my parents as they smiled and lifted their shoulders. A meeting had been called once I had made my intentions clear, and as we all sat in the bishop's study there was just a slight tension in the air but I was confident my parents would support me and I wasn't disappointed..
'Well, he is of age now to make these kinds of decisions for himself, he has saved up his money for the fare, and it's not as though he doesn't know what to expect,' my stepfather offered mildly, 'His family there will look out for him and besides, let him have the break he deserves before he hits the serious study.'
The bishop looked dubious but he could hardly refuse. The church

and those within it who were privy to my special status regarded me possessively, and as their most precious protégée no unnecessary risks must be taken that would endanger me in any way, but I was nothing less than determined and had already stated my case and now sat quietly as my proposal was discussed.

'Jonas is not someone who can be kept in a gilded cage. His calling is unique and you must trust him to own his instincts when something draws him like this. We can only give him support when he feels unsure, and allow him to master the wings that God has given him.'

It was my mother, and with a subtle reminder that was not lost on all present and I could have hugged her as I saw the bishop's shoulders slump.

'Very well,' he said, 'and at least we can take comfort that you will not be going alone. I understand your friends are to accompany you?'

'Yes, although I don't think I could've refused them if I tried,' and I smiled at the memory of their equal enthusiasm to join me on what they called an adventure, and their unmitigated excitement when their parent's agreement to provide the fare.

'*Africa,*' Menna had breathed her eyes bright, 'everyone goes to Europe or Australia on their year out, but we're going to *Africa* ...'

I think it might have been at that moment I fell in love with her. It was as enthralling as it was unexpected, but that my feelings for her had developed beyond friendship there could be no doubt, and as my mind began to dwell on this subject for the umpteenth time my stepfather's voice pulled me back into the room.

'The twins have proven themselves to be good friends, and sensible with it,' he said pointedly, 'in fact I can't think of anyone else I'd rather have watching his back, except for us – and you, of course, Your Worshipfulness,' He winked and the bishop gave a sigh of mock exasperation.

'Alright, you have persuaded me, Rhys, although I'll have to reassure the board that Jonas won't be taking off across the continent never to return!' He turned to me then, his manner grave, the grey eyes soft with appeal. 'You are very precious to us, my son, and it is a heavy gift you bear, we know. But we are also aware that you are young and untested, so all I ask is that you call in to us twice a week and stay away from anything that may lure you from the path.'

Menna's laughing face rose up before my eyes, but I met his gaze levelly for there could be no danger in having strong feelings, surely, and there in that flawed thought I made my first mistake.

'I give you my word, Father,' I replied solemnly, but there was a flare in my stomach; not just for my in anticipation of this trip, but that Menna would also be coming and that I dared hope she might feel the same.

'Then I give you my blessing, and may God keep you safe from all harm, my son,'

I bowed my head to receive his blessing, aware of my parents eyes upon me all but bursting with pride, and as soon as the formalities were over and the final arrangements made, I slipped out to where Steff and Menna were waiting and quickly gave them the news.

'So you can go! *We can go?* Oh wow, I can't believe this is happening, it's going to be *great,* isn't it Menna!' Steffan was doing a little dance as he punched the air. 'Best we get our jabs sorted then and some serious sun-block, I'm thinking, sis!'

But Menna wasn't listening. Her eyes were looking up at me and there was an almost shy smile on her lips that told me all I needed to know, and my heart did a deep sea dive never to return.

Chapter 9

That was my first summer of love and it was to be my last. People like me are not deigned to live easy lives, and had I known that then, I would have spared us all the heartbreak. But I was young and love is reckless, and in spite of the sanctity of my position, there was in me, nevertheless, the desire to be no different to any man who had feelings for a lovely young woman, and Menna had well and truly stolen my heart.
At this point it was unspoken, of course, but there were weeks ahead of us in a wild and exotic country and suddenly overcome with shyness myself, I was happy for things to naturally take their course. If her brother knew what was blossoming between us he gave no indication, and we were a merry crew as we disembarked in Ethiopia airport, the twins all but agog at their surroundings.
As before Samuel came to collect me and greeted my friends as though they were long-lost family. As we exchanged the most heartfelt of hugs he murmured softly, 'Welcome home, *Bekele*, welcome home. How pleased I am to see you. It has been too long, *too long!*'
Unlike the first time when I visited with my mother, the journey in the car was noisy and animated as both Steff and Menna *oohed* and *aahed*, my uncle was only too pleased to add to their delight, and by the time we'd reached the village celebration was already underway in honour of our coming and I felt a lump rise in my throat.
All of my life I had been stared at and talked about and as much as I was now armoured against it, here I felt my natural defences slip away as my father's kin pulled me joyously into their midst. From the corner of my eye I could see the twins equally being greeted as we were ushered into the main hut where the elders were waiting.
'Ah, Jonas, so you have returned to us.'
I knelt to receive their blessing and then stood up and brought Steff and Menna forward.
Their air of awed respect was evident as they were formally

welcomed and then water was brought for us to wash before the feasting began.

Some hours later as the fires were lit and the excitement died down, Menna turned to me, her face alight with pleasure.

'Jonas, this is so wonderful, like nothing I could ever have expected! And your people are so welcoming, so lovely, and *so* proud of you!' she leaned in suddenly and placed a hand on my arm added, 'and as they should be.'

There was a warmth in her eyes I'd not seen before and as words rose unbidden to my lips a shadow fell across us and I looked up to see Samuel.

'A word, Jonas, if you please?' he said smiling. 'Excuse us, please, young lady,'

Feeling slightly perplexed I followed him outside and it was only when we far from earshot that he turned to me, the smile now replaced by a solemn look.

'What is it? What's wrong, uncle?'

'Perhaps I am wrong but then I know a look of love when I see one; how long have you and the girl had feelings for each other, Jonas?'

'Why, uncle, you say it as though it is a bad thing.' There was just the merest edge to my voice but I couldn't help it.

'It *is* a bad thing,' he countered quietly.

'But why, uncle, why? We are friends, *good* friends; nothing has ... '

'What I just saw between you was far from *nothing* Jonas!' He creased his brow, concern marring the handsome features. 'You are set on a path that requires more training, much more! And you are off to new places of study, are you not, once this free-time is over? And how much do you think having such feelings will affect your concentration?'

'I have a right to love and to have feelings. Even my father had *that!*' I said mulishly.

Samuel reached out and placed a hand on my shoulder.

'Jonas, look at me! Of course you are. I am not saying not ever; I am just saying, *not now*,' His voice softened and I felt a lightness that had been in my heart begin to dissipate for I knew he spoke the truth, but rebellion had stirred within my depths; a feeling quite unknown to me.

'You have grown into a fine young man, a handsome young man, and many will find you attractive as so you will them, but when the time is right a partner must be chosen with the greatest of care, *the greatest of care*!' He emphasized, 'And let me tell you that were many women who threw themselves at your father, but he bided his time until the right one came along; and so she did, your mother. But you must also know that he was nearly thirty, Jonas, before he allowed himself the fruits of love, for well he knew the dangers of distraction therein and, well ... you know the rest.'

There rose between us the memory of my father setting off into the bush, never to be seen again, and how the power of his calling had left his wife a widow with me little more than a babe on her hip. Our lives had changed forever from that moment, and if it hadn't been for a rumbustious ex-miner from half a world away who, too, had heard the call of God, where would my mother and I be now?

I often asked myself that question and would envisage all kinds of scenarios, but it was upon asking my mother one day for her thoughts on the subject that the directness of her response left me in no doubt.

'We would probably be a pile of bleached bones in the desert, Jonas,' she had said an odd light in her eyes, 'for the famine was so far-reaching, it was only by the grace of God we made it into the camp that day - and into the sights of Rhys Llewellyn. In that itself was a miracle, for we were amidst an endless flood of desperate humanity and with thousands arriving every day, disease and death were rife, and there were many, sadly who did not make it.'

She had cried then. Long silent tears that shuddered her body, and unaccustomed to seeing my mother so unusually upset I could only think to take her in my arms as I wondered if my father's bones lay somewhere in the desert baking in the sun, and shed a few tears of my own.

I bowed my head and then Samuel was speaking again.

'I am not saying that you cannot enjoy a stolen kiss or two that sometimes comes with friendship, but what I am saying is to guard your heart and retain your focus. Ensure that your schooling comes first, Jonas, and then, if this Menna is still around and willing to wait - not only will you be sure of her intentions, but you will also be sure of your own.'

My head whipped up at that.

'But my intentions *are* honourable, uncle! I would never disrespect Menna, nor try to take advantage of her feelings for me, and besides, we feel the same.'

'Which is why I see fit to give you fair warning, Jonas. You are young, and you are bright, but we both know that whatever happens between you and this girl can bear no more weight than that of a feather,' he leaned into me and his voice took on a warning tone. 'Allow yourself the time that is needed to hone and learn all of your skills; and then, when you are fully adept in all of God's arts can you look perhaps to some earthly comforts.'

His words went deep and I knew I would have to master myself in the weeks ahead and regard it as almost a test of endurance, and as we made our way back to the main company I forced a smile in response to Menna's worried look.

It was part of what attracted her to me. Her uncanny way of sensing my mood and yet not being intrusive. Her sensitivity, her enthusiasm for life, and her natural ability to make people feel at ease. But my uncle's words had driven deep and I made a conscious decision to ignore how the light from the fires lit embers in her hair, the curve of her throat when she laughed at something. Yet I would enjoy her company, nevertheless, and in the way that I had always done, not realising in my naiveté that love has a way of bending all the rules, and that we are at heart, creatures of passion who will always play with fire of a different kind in the name of love.

The twins were keen to explore the area and learn more of the local culture, and Gondar with its plethora of palaces, churches and castles kept us busy as Samuel took on the role of our guide. They were dusty, hot but happy days as we went from site to site returning in the evenings to spicy stews and talks around the campfire.

I, too, enjoyed these excursions having not previously had the chance to explore these places, but there was also a part of me that longed to return to the mountains. So when I suggested an overnight hike up into the Simien heights the twins jumped at it.

'That would be wonderful!' enthused Steffan, 'as long as your uncle doesn't mind, of course.'

'It would be my pleasure,' said Samuel, 'there is a well-used route used by holiday-makers that will suit us well enough and it will make a pleasant change from all of the noise of the city.'

I caught his eye and he nodded imperceptibly. There would be no sojourn up to our sacred spot, just an ordinary hike and before the sun had fully risen the next morning we were all up packed and ready.

'Have you got your hats – and sunscreen? It can get really hot in the mountains.'

'Of course, don't fuss, Jonas!' admonished Menna, 'unless of course you mean the other kind of hot,' she added in an undertone and I turned away pretending not to hear.

It was the first time she had openly referred to any feelings between us and her boldness surprised me. But then Menna could be full of surprises which was part of her appeal, and as we took up the trail and fell in step behind Samuel and Steffan, I pointed out the various landmarks and the stories behind them.

'Do you ever get homesick?' she asked suddenly.

'What, for Wales? Why, yes, of course but ...'

'No. For here.'

I shrugged.

'In a strange way, sometimes yes. But I have no memory of it other than the first visit when I came out with my mother.'

'So you wouldn't move back here, then? If you had the choice, I mean.' I could feel her eyes on me and once again I wondered how much she knew – or speculated upon.

'Who knows where any of us will end up, Menna,' I replied, 'the world is a very big place and I have no other plans other than where God decides to send me.'

We walked in silence for some moments as the sun rose behind us and began to warm our backs.

'Then it could be a lonely life, I'm thinking,' she said stopped to heave her backpack into a more comfortable position. 'Both me and Steffan have kind of got used to having you around. It'll be strange when we go back to Bangor and you won't be there.'

'But only for a little while, Menna, and of course we'll keep in touch.'

'Will you?'

For the second time that morning I feigned an air of ignorance and adopting a light tone said, 'Will I what?'
She gave me a playful poke in the ribs.
'You know exactly what I mean, Jonas Llewellyn, so don't you play the innocent with me!'
I grinned at her in return, 'Of course I will, I wouldn't *dare not!*'
We both laughed as Samuel and Steffan looked around and then stopped waiting for us to catch up.
'I don't know what you two are laughing about,' Steffan said teasingly, 'but it's starting to get really warm and we haven't even reached the foothills yet, so I'd save your breath if I were you!'
His face was pink with exertion and we paused for a few minutes as he fussed with his pack. I looked to Menna and watched as she took a deep drink from her water-bottle and never thought she looked more beautiful than she did in that moment. My heart swooped and I knew deep within it there would be no other woman for me.
Samuel was also watching and I saw his brow furrow as we set off back up the track and after a while he turned and called out to Menna.
'Young lady, why not swap places and come up here and walk with me for a while! Your brother is so full of questions I think it would be a good test of my nephew's knowledge for him to share how much *he* has learnt.'
I suppressed the twinge of resentment that rose within me. That my uncle meant well, I knew, but it was more difficult than I thought to control my feelings and for all of the uniqueness about me, I was still a virile young man and not immune to the desires that rose within me.
'What are you looking so serious about?'
Steffan had fallen into step with me and I made a conscious effort to pull myself together. So far there had been no indication that Steffan knew of the growing feelings between me and Menna. But then they were twins and there wasn't much they didn't know about each other and surely he couldn't be that blind?
I pushed these thoughts aside and favoured him with a wide grin.
'Well, I was just wondering whether I'll have to carry you to the top you're that red, Steffan!'
'And I wouldn't say no!' he retorted, '*Iesu Grist*, Jonas, your uncle sets a pace, doesn't he! How much further do you think?'

The twins were both visibly relieved when we stopped to rest beneath the cool shade of some trees. The heat was now at its height and everyone reached gratefully for their water bottles as Samuel passed round fruit and *injera,* and soon we had eaten our fill and drowsed comfortably propped against our packs.

The heat shimmered across the valley as an eagle circled lazily up in the thermals. The skies were azure for as far as the eye could see as the mountains spread out before us.

'It is so beautiful here and I can't stop looking at the view, but my eyes are so heavy I could sleep now,' murmured Menna but her yawn was interrupted as Steffan suddenly sat forward saying, 'What's that? What's that moving? Oh look, it's a troop of baboons!'

Samuel and I were on our feet immediately and sure enough there was a small group picking their way slowly along a ridge towards us.

'What's wrong? What's up? They're not going to attack us, are they?' Menna was now wide awake and there was alarm in her voice as she scrambled to her feet.

'No, no,' said my uncle, although I could tell by his tone that he wasn't really sure, 'but they are known to be unpredictable and we are in their territory after all ...'

I could feel myself tensing as the memory of that fateful fight came back and almost sub-consciously eased Menna behind me as Steffan swiftly rose and joined his sister.

'Just stay quiet now, not a word.'

I had my staff before me as did Samuel as we watched the baboons approach. There were about a dozen of them and they had seen us, of course, pausing just briefly before moving down from the ridge as though to give us wide berth and as they drew nearer I heard Menna exclaim, 'Oh look! One of them has got a broken arm, poor thing!' and I felt myself go cold.

Chapter 10

It couldn't be! *Surely!* Swiftly my eyes sought and found those of my one-time assailant as it brought up the rear, and it appeared to pause momentarily as though it too had recognised me. I was amazed that it had been allowed to stay with the group and felt pity for its obvious demise in the hierarchy. But it had survived courtesy of the large young male at the head that regarded disdainfully.
I felt the breath slowly leave my body as Samuel's shoulders relaxed. The baboons were merely passing through; we just happened to be near their usual route.
Humans were a frequent visitor to the Simien Mountains, it was in a National Park after all and tourists a common sight to the local wildlife, but just seeing my old adversary again had reminded me of the dangers that my path would invite and fear touched on me for anyone close to me, including my friends.
We all remained watching until they were out of sight disappearing down the path but it wasn't until later when we'd found a quiet spot to camp that Menna broached the subject of their appearance and how it had affected me.
Steffan had gone off with Samuel to refill the water-bottles from a nearby spring as we gathered wood for the fire. Already the air was cooling as the sun began to dip amidst an array of golden colours but Menna had no interest in the sunset, and as I laid down an assortment of sticks she drew my attention with a touch on my sleeve.
'Are you alright now, Jonas?'
I looked down at her quizzically and she gave a tentative smile.
'I don't mean to pry, but the way in which you and your uncle reacted I thought for a moment we were in serious danger and that they were going to come at us. I know that Steffan did too. But it was actually *you* that gave me the most cause for alarm.'
I said nothing and waited for her to go on.
'You changed. It was like a switch had gone on, and I know that this is going to sound really crazy, but it was as though you came to life, but in *another* way, and ...'

'*Hey!* Haven't you two got that fire going yet?'
It was Steffan. As he came towards us in mock-stagger under the weight of the bottles I murmured, 'Later.' Before kneeling down and getting the fire going.
We had supper watching the last light of day as it receded swiftly from the sky, and just before it disappeared completely Menna jumped to her feet and turned to me saying, 'Come on! Let's say *nos da* to the sunset and send our love to Wales. Steffan, are you coming?'
Her brother waved a weary hand.
'Are you kidding? I'm done in, sis, and there's no way I'm leaving this cosy fire.'
Jonas stood up feeling his uncle's eyes on him and reaching for his blanket indicated that Menna did the same, and wrapped up like two mountain nomads they made their way over to the bluff and into the last of the light.
As soon as they were out of earshot Menna spoke.
'When I was little I can remember my *nain* telling me about an old woman who lived not far from the shores of *Llyn Tegid*. By all accounts she was a wise, kind-hearted woman who minded her own business, but some said she worshipped the old gods and had special powers and could throw a full grown man into the lake if you upset her. Well, you know how it is ... people make up stories and word gets passed along; only in this case, my *nain,* who was a young girl herself at the time, was passing by the lake when she saw the old woman having an argument with some strangers. My *nain* wasn't sure what the row was about only that the old lady seemed very angry and that there was lots of shouting going on.'
Somewhere above us an owl gave a small hoot but I kept my gaze on Menna as she looked out to the night sky.
'Things were getting really heated and then all of a sudden the old woman threw off her cloak and with her stick set about the men like a fury and sent them packing. But what makes this story so unbelievably incredible; is that my *nain* swore on the bible, *and* her life that it was true; the strangers involved were no less than five fully-grown men, and that the old woman herself was well over ninety years of age!'

She turned to me then.

'And so what do you think of that, Jonas?'

But before I could speak she laid a finger on my lips and lowering her voice further said, 'You don't have to answer because I know, 'she nodded imperceptibly, 'I've always known. Because people like you don't come around often and we Welsh can also be well-versed in what some might call the *llygad ysbryd*.'

She removed her finger and stepped back her expression unreadable.

'Don't worry, Jonas, your secret is safe with me.'

'Menna, I ...'

'No, there's no need to explain. Today merely confirmed it, for I sensed the shift in energy as soon as those baboons appeared and I know that Steffan felt it, too, although he'll already have forgotten it such is the extent of his attention span!'

We smiled at each other in recognition of knowledge and a special moment shared.

'I just wanted you to know, and that you can trust me, although your uncle has other ideas, I feel... ' She deliberately left the sentence hanging.

'He only wishes to look out for me. There are some things you can't know, Menna.' I said gently.

'I understand.'

The sun had slipped below the horizon as the first stars came out casting her face into a pale shadow and once again the owl gave voice only this time as a mournful cry.

'Will you wait for me?'

I hardly dared ask the question but it fell from my lips as a whisper of hope and my heart soared as I saw her nod her head, and for the first time in my life I felt pure joy and blindly, without thinking, caught her up in my arms as our mouths found each other and came together in a passionate kiss.

Inwardly I marvelled at how soft her lips were, how pliant, and I felt a rising hunger as her body's heat seeped into mine. The blood rushed to my head and for the heartbeat of a moment nothing else mattered. For the first time I was holding a girl in my arms and with so much love it was as though something deep within me had ignited and I was fully flamed with fire.

Jonas
Like a merest echo I heard his voice in my head, but it was strong enough to bring me to my senses and with infinite gentleness I lowered Menna down as her eyes sought mine and questioned.
'Menna ... we cannot. I dare not ...' And to hide the awkwardness of the moment I added, 'but as for that being my first kiss, I could not have wished for better!'
'I was your first kiss? Really?' Her pleasure was obvious and gazing up at me she whispered, 'then let it not be our last!'
I looked at her longingly but could feel unseen eyes upon us and I knew my uncle was in some way listening and that he knew, as I did now, how close I had come to losing control.
Ah Menna, if only you knew.
'I cannot. I'm sorry, *cariad*,' and as I drew back further I saw the hurt expression before she masked it with a bright smile.
'Which is why we must wait, and I understand, Jonas, really I do... but it's going to be hard, isn't it? Harder perhaps than we both had thought it ever would be.'
We stared at each other in the dying light, and as the chill crept around us I now understood why Samuel had warned me, for having brought my feelings out into the open meant I knew the strength of them, and they were powerful enough to perplex me.
I never thought, being as different as I was that anyone would ever fall in love with me; much less that I would ever find someone and do the same. Having been stared at all my life for no other reason than how I looked and the colour of my skin, the inevitable name-calling that came with it had instilled in me long ago a quiet acceptance that somebody as different as me *couldn't* be loved. And as I gazed down into the eyes of this lovely young woman I saw the truth of it and drew her in to me protectively.
'That story you told me about with the men and the old woman. It was more familiar to me than you could ever know and yes, there are people in this world who have a certain light as there are those who make it their business to try and put it out. Which is why we must remain separate, until the time is right and my studies are complete.'
'What studies are those, Jonas? I know you have been granted a special place at the Vatican in which to finish your education – but

then it is no normal education you are receiving, is it?'
I made no immediate answer. Both she and Steff had been round me long enough to understand that the type of ministry I was being prepared for was not a conventional one, but neither had really come out and said anything; until now, and the less she or Steff knew the better.
'I will tell you, one day perhaps, when I am in a position to, Menna. I give you my word on that. But until then, I will keep you firmly in my heart and with hope that you will find the wait worth it.'
'Jonas Llewellyn, one of the things I love about you is that you're just too modest by far!' Menna hugged me to her fiercely, 'you are a beautiful man, both inside and out, and I would be *twp* to miss the chance of being with someone like you! So *yes*, I will wait, and *yes,* it will be so worth it, for the very fact our love has been built on a strong friendship, and whatever happens between us we will always be friends, won't we, Jonas?'
I bent down and kissed the top of her head.
'Always, Menna. But there's just one other thing.'
She pulled back and looked up at me questioningly.
'I think, I know that Steffan will be alright with us, but what about your parents?'
'What about them?'
I gave a small laugh.
'Menna, it's one thing to have a friend like me hanging around and to be honest, they have never been anything but pleasant. They may, however, become less accepting once they realise that they'll be having a black giant for a son-in-law!'
'Let me worry about them and they will have time enough to come round to that idea, believe me! Now, a kiss and then another because we both know that your uncle watches us like a hawk and I want to treasure this moment because in two days we will be leaving and then Lord knows when we'll see each other again.'
'It won't be as long as you ...' and then my words were cut off as she leaned up and pulled my head down to hers, and as the owl hooted its disapproval I lost myself for some moments in a passion I never knew existed.
Swiftly I pulled away as something growled deep in the night.

'Come on, we'd best get back, it's nearly dark and we are far from the fire.'

And my staff! I thought inwardly and cursed my stupidity for having left it back in camp but it was a clear warning of the dangers of distraction and I vaguely took note.

With one arm around Menna I hurried us back towards the glow of the fire as another growl came out of the darkness, nearer this time.

'What is it? Is it the baboons?' Menna's voice remained steady although there was fear in it.

'No.'

The story of my father being stalked by a mountain lion during his initiation period flashed through my mind, but I held my peace and as soon as we reached the safety of the camp I snatched up my staff. Steffan was already fast asleep and snoring gently curled up tight in his blanket, but Samuel was awake and alert. To my surprise he remained seated as I paced the perimeter of light thrown by the fire. I had expected him to join me.

'Trouble, Jonas?' he said quietly.

Menna lowered herself down slowly next to him her eyes wide and darting through the darkness.

'I'm not sure. Just something prowling about, I think.'

Samuel stoked up the fire and threw on more wood as Menna huddled in her blanket.

'Don't worry, miss, nothing will come too close, not with this fire, but just to reassure you and to doubly make sure, Jonas will be happy to keep watch for the night, won't you, Jonas?'

It was a punishment of sorts, I knew, and I accepted it stoically.

I had done the one thing I had been warned over and over not to do, and that was to leave myself unprotected. But what made it worse was that I had endangered Menna with no thought to the consequences.

Before rolling himself up in his blanket my uncle had given me a meaningful look that said everything, and as I stood and looked out into the night lit by a thousand stars, my mind returned again and again to that kiss and I vowed then and then I would never again be so careless.

But the Devil is more cunning than I would ever give him credit for and as always when he plays a rogue hand, by the time you realise he's outsmarted you, it's usually, invariably too late.

Chapter 11

It was a muted flight on the way back after an emotional farewell. Steffan was especially introspective for we'd thought it only fair to put him in the picture as to how Menna and I felt about each other and it had taken him by surprise.
'I knew you two always got along, but I must have been walking around blind not to have noticed how things had progressed from that! Are you sure this isn't some kind of holiday romance thing? And so how is this going to work anyway, with Jonas half-way across the world!'
He was initially miffed that he hadn't noticed anything, but then was cautiously pleased once he realised we were serious enough to want to wait for each other.
'Can't say this isn't going to cause a stir within the family, but I'll give you my support, for what it's worth. Mam's going to go through the roof though when she hears though,' he retorted to Menna.
'I know,' she said smugly, 'but she'll have two years to get used to the idea. Jonas and I intend to be together, and once he's finished his studies we can take it from there.'
My parents received the news with even less enthusiasm.
'It's not because we're not happy for you, Jonas,' my mother had said earnestly, 'it's just that we think you're too young to tie yourself down. There is plenty of time for you to find someone.'
'But not like Menna. She knows me, she trusts me. We trust each other.'
'How much does she know you, though, Jonas ... I mean, *really know you?*'
My stepfather was looking at me keenly and I met his stare squarely.
'She knows me well enough. Enough to realise that I'll be no ordinary man of the cloth, and she accepts that, in fact she accepts everything about me, and Lord knows I'd be hard-pushed to find anyone like her that does.'
'So you are in love,' my mother said softly, 'My son, my Jonas, finally growing up and knowing his own heart.' and she gave a small

smile.

'At eighteen!' Rhys snorted and glowered beneath his brows, 'I barely knew how to fart in the wind at that age!'

'Ah, yes,' said my mother soothingly, 'but you knew how to fight and you were out and about most weekends then, weren't you, my love – before God called you to a higher purpose, of course,' she added sweetly and he glared at her.

'Never mind that! What I'm trying to say Abeba, is that this boy – eighteen or not, he's still a boy in my eyes – has such responsibility upon him it wouldn't be fair on the girl. Have you thought about that, Jonas?'

'Your father has a point, and as pleased as I am that you've found somebody who loves you as you are, there are certain considerations to take into place, and as much as Menna has always struck me as open-minded as the next – everyone had their limits, Jonas.'

I gazed at them both with a barely-suppressed exasperation. We had never really had words before for I was by nature, quiet and respectful with no wish to cause disagreement. But now, here I was, in the throes of first love and I found I had a stubborn streak of a different kind.

'I will wait for her, as she intends to wait for me. In the eyes of the law I am legally an adult and I will love who I choose. God, I am sure, would not deny me that..?'

My stepfather looked at me as though assessing me for the first time as my mother threw up her hands.

'Very well, as you choose, I can see that you are determined on this. Just be careful, Jonas, that is all we ask.'

It wasn't the blessing I wanted but it was enough, and when I left on to the next stage of my training it was with assurances that I would write and call often and so began the next part of my journey.

I was sorry to leave Bangor. I had enjoyed my time there exploring the local history, and I would never forget that day at Penmon when its Holy Man appeared and shared a universal secret with me. As promised I had held it tight, but the day would come when all would be revealed and more. Until then, I had more knowledge to accrue, more study to undertake, more secrets to uncover. That I was a traveller at heart soon became apparent once my confidence grew, and with it a growing hunger to know more about my unique heritage and what lay ahead.

With the exception of my parents and high-ranking officials within the Diocese, everyone thought I had won a scholarship to study exclusively within the Vatican for a short period. What they didn't know was that I had been invited to Rome specifically and by none other than the Pope himself.

For someone who had been plucked from starvation and given a new life in a strange new country, to suddenly find oneself about the enter the splendour of the Vatican was so surreal that at times I had to pinch myself.

Not even my time up in the mountains with my uncle Samuel had felt as other-worldly as this, but thankfully Einion had been allowed to accompany me and I was incredibly grateful for that.

We were housed in the nearby *Hotel Columbus* that had once been a medieval monastery dating from the First Crusade. Indeed it still housed the office for the *Equestrian Order of the Holy Sepulchre of Jerusalem*, a religious military order from that period which added to the whole mystique.

'I don't know about you, Jonas, but I *really feel* as though I'm in Rome!' my old tutor had enthused as we ate breakfast with al fresco's on the ceiling, and I felt a *frisson* of excitement run through me for I knew what he meant.

We had been issued with an instruction to present ourselves at the *Porta di Sant'Anna*, the business entrance to the Vatican, and catching sight of the elaborate Swiss guards as we approached suitably filled me with awe. They checked the proffered paperwork thoroughly and eyed the great wooden cross around my neck before looking up at me questioningly.

With the help of a skilled joiner back in my father's village, the sacred staff when it was folded in repose had now been strongly threaded so it could be worn around my neck. To the innocent eye it looked nothing more than an exceptionally large cross, although some might say excessive, but it was a means to keeping it close to me at all times, and I wouldn't go anywhere without it.

That, my tattoos and great height combined with my colour meant

that I was stared at even more, and having passed the first phase of ecclesial training, my regular attire was also now the standard clerical frock. My appearance was obviously troubling the guards and I sensed their reluctance to let me pass, despite our letter of introduction.
'Is there a problem here?'
An official swept out from the interior like a great bird of prey, his black robes flapping and a crimson cap set atop the balding head. He glanced at us keenly his eyes resting on me for some moments before taking the proffered paperwork which he scanned quickly.
'Yes, yes, this is all in order. They may enter. Welcome Jonas, and Mr Lewis, I am Father Roberto. Please, follow me!'
Einion and I exchanged a bemused glance at the fact I'd been addressed informally. There had been no 'Mr Llewellyn' for me and an indication to expect the unexpected.
We left the guards at the entrance and were ushered into a wood-panelled office where we were greeted by two clerks whose eyes widened when they saw me. Sat behind an ornate glass screen it was their job to check all documentation of visiting guests before issuing a pass with the Pope's crest.
I could feel Einion's rising excitement as we then followed the official towards a door at the other end of the room. It brought us out on to a walkway that ran the length of the Apostolic Palace. Here there were more Swiss guards, stood silently like elaborate toy soldiers at their posts as we realised with a sense of awe that we were finally inside the Vatican proper.
It was like another world as all manner of people and officials hurried about their daily tasks. Nuns, clerics, maintenance men, florists, we took it all in as a few glanced our way or stopped to stare and then we were whisked away into another part of the Palace as a hush descended leaving the bustle behind.
Our guide led us through a warren of passages before finally coming to a halt outside a large wooden door with the most beautiful carvings. He gave a sharp rap before turning the handle and ushering us inside.
Several high-ranking Vatican officials in various codes of dress fell silent as we came into the plushly appointed room, and there was a

pregnant pause as we all took each other's measure.
'May I introduce Jonas Llewellyn and his tutor from the Diocese of Bangor the Reverend Einion Lewis.'
They bowed their heads as we bowed ours as further introductions were made before we were all seated at the large antique table between us and refreshments offered.
Accepting a cool glass of water I sat back crossing my legs and waited. I was aware that Einion's prior anticipation had given way to extreme nervousness and I had to suppress a smile as I heard his cup give a small rattle on the saucer.
I was only eighteen but old for my years. I had lived all of my life under the scrutiny of every person I had ever met. Been regarded as, and often called, a freak of all persuasions, but my training had instilled in me a complete lack of fear. Not just through my formidable knowledge of the most ancient form of martial art; but through an unshakeable inner strength that had always sustained me in my darker moments. With such a firmness of faith, fear had no foothold, and so I faced the sea of intent faces before me serenely as the leading official began to read from a long list of questions.
The next part of my journey had begun.

It was some hours later after a delicious luncheon that Einion and I were escorted from the building and back out into the sunny plaza. It had been a gruelling few hours, mentally, as well as emotionally, as every aspect of my life, parentage and heritage was held up before me and addressed at length.
I was also requested to demonstrate some of my other more hidden talents which I duly did, much to their amazement, and by the time all of the questioning and testing were complete there was a palpable air of satisfaction as the officials ticked boxes and murmured amongst themselves.
'We will be in touch,' said Father Roberto shaking our hands warmly. He was less formal now that the meeting was over and the validity of my unique status seemingly confirmed. 'Enjoy the sights while you are here, the day is young yet!'
With this advice in mind we made our way to St. Peter's Square and mingled with the crowds before finding a quiet cafe in one of the

many backstreets. Being careful not to be overheard we began to dissect the day's events.

'I have to be honest with you, Jonas,' Einion's honest face was creased with concern, 'when we walked into that room and the way they stared at us, I really had a feel of what it must've been like to been before the Inquisition!'

I gave a small chuckle, 'Yes, it was a bit like that, but then I don't suppose it's often they meet a six foot four Welshman from Ethiopia!'

'And still growing!' observed Einion and took a small sip of his espresso. 'So tell me, Jonas, how long do you think it will be until you meet the holy man himself?'

'Which one?' I countered, and when he looked at me askance I shook my head. 'No matter, Einion, and in answer to your question, soon, sooner than you may think.'

'What, is this something you know, or something you feel, or..?'

'Both, but then both are one and the same to me.'

My old tutor gazed at me thoughtfully for some moments. He had always struggled with the whole concept of my clairsentience, but then as the son of a vicar he had always been immersed in just one line of teaching which made the choice of him as my tutor all the more unusual.

But he was discreet and dependable, and that counted for much under the circumstances. He was also unmarried and so wholly committed to the church that he'd accepted the role of my companion stoically, despite the differences between us. Indeed he was so amenable that if he'd been asked to accompany me into the depths of the Arctic he wouldn't have demurred.

The message came that very evening, hand-delivered by a stern-faced official and from the Pope himself. We were to present ourselves promptly at 10 am the following morning; His Holiness was most keen to make my acquaintance, and I in turn, was intrigued at the prospect of meeting this exceptional man. I knew that he had expressed a great desire of bringing all religions together, and had demonstrated a humble strength of spirit not to be underrated in the face of current world events. He was, to say the least, something of a spiritual enigma.

Einion chortled delightedly upon hearing the news.

'I can't believe I'm going to meet the Pope! I mean, *the Pope!* I know we're not of the same denomination, Jonas, but it still a great honour and *you!* Aren't you nervous? How many people would sell their soul just to go into the inner sanctum of the Vatican, never mind a private audience with His Holiness!'

I smiled at his barely-suppressed glee for he was not a man given to such bouts of enthusiasm, but then the staidness of his usual world had been thrown on its head, and the very atmosphere of Rome itself had obviously worked its magic and I'd have been lying if I said I was immune.

The people, the language, the history, the smells, it was all so ebullient and colourful to what we were used to.

I thought then of Menna and how she would love the special ambience; perhaps when life was more certain I could bring her here to sample the delights, and then Einion drew me back with a question to which I did not know the answer.

'Do we bow, do we shake his hand, or do we simply dip our knees? How on earth do you greet the Pope! What exactly is the protocol?'

I looked at Einion bemused.

'I have absolutely no idea, but I'm sure we'll be told beforehand,'

'Ah yes, *wrth gwrs, wrth gwrs ...*' he slapped a hand to his head comically, 'it's all just so extraordinary, Jonas, just so ... so *extraordinary!*'

And it was, too, for when we were brought into the Pope's presence, he wasn't alone, and even I, who was ever rarely shaken, felt my eyes widen in wonder as I took in who also stood before us, and then the doors were shut firmly behind us.

'Welcome to the Vatican.'

Einion and I exchanged the briefest of glances before moving forward and kneeling before the white clad figure as his companion benignly looked on. Although we were not of the Catholic faith we had pre-agreed to follow protocol as a matter of respect. My standing was tenuous enough and it was important I made a good impression.

We kissed the ring of St Peter murmuring your 'Your Holiness' before rising and standing somewhat awkwardly before these two great spiritual leaders whose eyes were intent upon me with a polite

but palpable curiosity.
The Pope then turned to his companion and formally introduced him although of course we knew who he was. We bowed our heads before being invited to sit on an ornate sofa as he took his on a rather grandly appointed chair. His guest took a lesser one as several officials hovered in the background as they discreetly kept a close eye on proceedings
'It is extremely fortuitous that my friend, the Dalai Lama should be visiting at this time, for we are both equally intrigued as to these gifts the good Lord had seen fit to bestow upon you. God willing, we would know more of you, Jonas and these ... blessings of which you have.'
I looked into the kindly face and saw a keen interest that was guarded nevertheless and began to relax, but my eyes kept going back to meet the inscrutable gaze of the spiritual leader of Tibet and marvelled that he should be here in the flesh.
Two great spiritual leaders, it was almost too much to take in! Einion, too, was in a state of awe, his mouth slightly agape, his hands tightly clasped in his lap as though he was afraid they'd take off.
I, in turn, was much more relaxed, but very much aware that the power of the Holy See and its far-reaching tentacles was not to be underestimated, and I was a lone man cast adrift upon an uncertain sea after all.
With the battles I knew I had before me, allies in high places could only be beneficial and besides, there was the matter of the Vatican library into which I hoped to have access.
'It would be my pleasure, your Holiness. Where would you like me to start?'
Pope John Paul sat back and steepled his fingers beneath his chin.
'Back where it all began; your family, your beginnings ... and please, be at ease, for you are among friends here and we would have you speak freely, my son. Perhaps, as a subject of particular interest to me, you could start with your connection to the man they called Simon the Sorcerer ...'

Chapter 12

I bowed my head. I was surprised at the Pope's direct line of approach. I had not expected him to go straightforward and it was some seconds before I gathered my thoughts. I knew I was under intense scrutiny; that every word, nuance and facial expression would be recorded during this interview. The Church of Rome was not known for its liberal views when it came to matters of spiritual diversity, and particular details of my heritage would be no exception. Yet despite this present Pope's conservative stance on many issues, his keenness to bring all faiths under one umbrella, however, was sincere and well known, and this gave me hope for a greater understanding and that he would look upon my lineage with an open mind.

I drew a deep breath and began.

'I was born in Ethiopia in a small village at the foot of the Simien Mountains. It was also the birthplace of my father - my mother came from Sudan. My line goes back to Shem, founder of the Semitic people who after the great flood settled predominantly in the Middle East, as you know. But a small contingent joined with the Lost Tribes of Dan in North Africa after they had been dispelled from Samaria because of their beliefs.'

I paused. Both the Pope and the Dalai Lama were rapt.

I went on.

'It was deemed easier for them to disappear quietly into the *Cush*, for land was plentiful there and like their counterparts, once disputes were settled with the indigenous peoples, they were allowed to settle and integrated peacefully thereafter with neighbouring tribes. There has been much written and speculated about the man they called Simon the Magician, I know, but it has been sworn to me by my family, both on the good book, and in blood, that my line is descended directly from Simon and that he was indeed a true man of God.'

The Pope shifted at that. Centuries of conjecture had determined that my ancestor, who had possessed the most amazing powers, had actually been in thrall to the Devil. But it was the history behind my ancestor and the founder of the Roman Church that was equally contentious, for records claimed that St. Peter had clashed with Simon the Magician and that the latter had caused great offence by offering money in exchange for more blessings after receiving the Holy Spirit. His reputation had preceded him, and despite having been baptised by St. Phillip, apparently he was not content and tried to bargain for more.

The Roman Church was no fan of the man they called Simon Magus, indeed Catholic theology used the term 'Simony' to condemn anyone trying to buy ordination or holy favours, but then I knew as well as anyone that testimony could be subverted when truth got in the way.

'It is difficult, I know, to equate someone who has been branded a heretic and a false prophet to be seen as anything less than unfavourable in the eyes of your church. But I swear before you on all that's holy, that he was a servant of the Divine, and that God had blessed him in an entirely different way, and the world, perhaps, was not ready for someone such as he was - which was why he disappeared as mysteriously as he came. But his line went on, his legacy lived on, albeit quietly, through the centuries, and so I stand before you as living proof of that.'

My boldness had hit a nerve as the Pope all but blanched and for the first time I saw the Dalai Lama's countenance change as the corner of his mouth twitched.

'You are very confident. Indeed for someone so young your confidence is almost as disturbing as it is...all-enveloping, my son.'

He was trying to recover and with some wit, I knew and I replied gently

'It is because I speak the truth, your Holiness. Word has been passed down generation after generation, as have the abilities with which God saw fit to bestow and has *continued* to bestow upon myself and my forefathers. And believe me when I say, I would not have the temerity to stand before you now, indeed *both* of you now, and make such assertion without the knowledge and the blessings of the one true God.'

'It is said that this man, Simon laid claim to having the light of the Divine within him; that he was as much a part of God as he was a

servant of God and that on this basis he would not kneel to St. Peter or any representative of God's grace with the assertion that he was God himself. A statement such as this can only be regarded as the greatest of blasphemies, for there is only one true Son of God, and so I would ask you now; what is your stance on this?'
I gave a small smile.
'Why, Your Holiness, we are all the children of God and as such are a part of him as much as he is a part of us, and so how can it be that we are not?'
My response was evidently not what he had been expecting and his mouth worked for some moments.
The Dalai Lama leaned forward. 'May I?'
The Pope nodded. There was a bewildered look in his eye.
'So tell me, young warrior of God; who or what is the one true God?' His manner was urbane is voice gentle with no hint of accusatory and I met his gaze squarely.
'It is not for the master to seek affirmation from the student, surely, your Holiness?' and was rewarded with another twitch of the lips before he sat back looking bemused. He understood me I knew instinctively, but it was not him who I needed to persuade and the Pope was struggling to maintain his composure.
'Jonas...my son... if what you say is true, then we must have evidence of this, you understand. We cannot turn a two thousand year old teaching on its head, a teaching that comes from the very book itself, on the sake of an oath, and although I know you have demonstrated your abilities before some of senior officials I still need...'
His mouth fell open and I heard Einion gasp beside me.
'What...what did you just do! How...'
The room fell silent. The only personage who wasn't displaying any kind of shock was the Dalai Lama who sat unperturbedly his hands steady on his lap.
'It's called levitation, your Holiness. I believe it was Simon the Magician's particular speciality. '
'Wha...*what?* I know what it is, but...' The Pope's cheeks had turned pink as his mind struggled to accept what he'd just seen.
I lifted my shoulders.
'My apologies if I startled you, Your Holiness, but you had asked for

proof and, well ...'

A murmuring started up at the back of the room where the officials remained in attendance and the Pope raised a hand restoring order. He had been momentarily shaken but a sudden glint in his eyes indicated a swift recovery and we all waited for him to speak.

'At one time such a display would've seen you despatched without delay to the stake,' he said gravely, 'and I would not have believed it if I had not witnessed it with my own eyes. But such abilities, it is said, are the work of the Devil and yet you have passed all tests, taken of the sacrament and sought only to be of service for the greater good ... and ... if it is as you say; that had God not wanted you to have these abilities then he would not, in his infinite wisdom, seen fit to give them to you, much less allow them to be used within the confines of his very house. And yet I would witness this extraordinary phenomenon once more, if you please ...'

This time I stood up and moved away before rising gracefully into the air and slowly turned a full circle before coming back down and resuming my seat.

The Dalai Lama was regarding me with an unreadable expression as for the second time the Pope's mouth dropped open and his officials fluttered excitedly in the background.

'Gentlemen!' he called sharply and they fell into silence, 'I would have you show some restraint, and be reminded that you are all under strict oath! Whatever happens or is said within this room remains in this room at the utmost discretion of each and every one of you.'

Suddenly he sighed deeply and seemed to almost slump in his chair. Gesturing to his guest he said soberly, 'I would be most grateful for your thoughts on this for I am, I will confess, quite at a loss for words. If what this young man says is true, then how can what is written in the holy book be so wrong? It goes against everything we have been taught about the integrity of this man ...' He shook his head before making a discreet sign of the cross.

The Dalai Lama took some moments to gather himself and I did not envy him his position.

It was one thing to be from a whole different sect where the principles of his religion flew in the face of even the most liberal views of Catholicism. And yet, here he was, not just as an invited guest of the

Holy See, but as an exceptionally privileged one for the fact he was even present at this meeting and allowed to bear witness. It spoke of a profound trust that went beyond the call of spiritual duty and I liked the Pope better for it.

'I will say only this,' he said quietly, 'that there are many things in this world that are open to misinterpretation, and that sometimes, such things are made to be deliberately so because man, as we know, will always aspire to do what he thinks is best. And from that we must draw comfort, even we are assailed by doubt; for it will be the resonance of what dwells within that will guide you, and so by listening to your own heart will you find the answer you seek.'

I bowed my head and wondered if he knew of the great revelation the saint on *Ynys Môn* had made known to me, but if he did, he was giving nothing away and I could no sooner draw from him as I could a rock.

I cast a quick glance towards Einion who was riveted in place. His eyes were like china-blue saucers and his mouth slack as you'd see on the face of a child at a circus. He had never seen me levitate before, and it came as much as a shock to him as it did to everyone else – except His Holiness from Tibet, of course, but then such things were not rare amidst the temples of Lhasa if rumour was to be believed.

An odd silence fell across the room like an unseen shadow as both the words of the Dalai Lama and my own sank in and it was colossal. For what we were both asserting, albeit in different ways, was that for two thousand years the Bible had cast aspersions upon an innocent man, damning his name forever amidst a litany of sin when all he had been, and had ever claimed to be, was a true man of God and that more importantly and staggering yet – *the Bible had got it wrong!*

'When I first went to the North of Wales to pursue the path that was laid out for me, I had cause to visit a small island that lay at the tip of the peninsula called *Ynys Mon*. At the easterly edge of the island is a place called Penmon Point and there you will find the remains of a priory and a holy well named after its founder, St. Seriol. And it was during this visit that this venerable old soul did me the honour of appearing to me...' I paused and you could have heard a pin drop. 'He came with counsel, and warnings of what lay ahead, and more miraculous still, he spoke to me in an archaic tongue that I was somehow able to understand. Among the many things he told me, he said that this meeting would come, and that doubt would be the biggest challenge followed by fear and that I was to impart a special message to your Holiness but for your ears only.'

The Pope stared at me for some moments, agonized uncertainty etched onto his features, his whole face now flushed with unspoken emotions. That he was deeply shaken there was no doubt, and when one of his aides stepped forward to speak he waved him away impatiently; the moment was nigh, the test was upon us like the final day of reckoning and in some unaccountable way, we all knew it. For here was I, the descendent of a much maligned and condemned disciple, stood before God's Apostle on earth as had Simon and Peter and in this very place, the encounter of which was recorded for all time within the annals of Holy Scripture and had been so for over two thousand years.

It was a sobering moment as it was a surreal one. Even the Dalai Lama had lost his serene look for we were all stood on a precipice that could go one way or the other.

The Holy Father's voice when it came was tight and cool with detachment.

'You have a private message for me ... from the spirit of a saint?'
I bowed my head.
'I do, Your Holiness.'

There was a long pause as the Pope appeared to be inwardly battling against a lifetime of conditioning and it was with a distinct heaviness of tone that he reached a decision.

'You may approach.'

Every eye on the room was on me as I rose and went across to where His Holiness sat like a stone statue, the folds of his robe pristinely white as the gold cross upon his chest gleamed brightly as though drawing me on, and I smelled just the hint of incense as I leaned down to his ear and then, in the softest of whispers I spoke.

The effect was as startling as it was immediate as tears sprang suddenly to the Pope's eyes and began to run down his face and I could see his whole body starting to tremble as my words went in. As soon as the message was delivered I stepped back and resumed my seat as the His Holiness cried out in Latin before lifting his cross and kissing it

His aides rushed forward darting accusatory looks at me as I took my seat next to Einion who looked fit to faint. But the Dalai Lama was nodding slowly as though he had heard every word.

The Pope waved his attendants back and then he looked directly at me in a way he had not before; this man who held the highest office in Christendom; lived in palatial splendour, exerted considerable ecclesiastical power, fawned upon and adored by Catholics the world over, and yet had never forgotten his humble beginnings nor the last words his mother spoke to him before she died.

And it was enough.

Drawing out a fine lawn handkerchief that was embroidered with the holy crest he mopped at his eyes as the church officials hovered near his chair confusion now replacing their alarm.

'Shall I call the guard, Your Holiness?' ventured one all but wringing his hands together.

'Indeed you shall not!' retorted the Pope, 'But what you will do is see that apartments are made ready for our guests, for in the light of these developments I will not have them lodged anywhere else but here in the Vatican.' He paused, 'If that meets with your approval, of course, Jonas?'

'Thank you, Your Holiness, that is most kind.'

'And convenient, for there is much still of which we must speak.' He began to issue orders, now very much back in control as his aides scurried from the room and then turning back to me said, 'I have done much apologising during my time in office and gladly, for the Church has, to my great sorrow been less than enlightened at times throughout its history, but *this*...' he shook his head wonderingly, 'is so sensitive a subject that I cannot see it ever becoming public for fear of what it might do to the church, not to mention you yourself, Jonas.' He spread his hands widely, 'Indeed such a revelation could be dangerous and make of you a target, my son and I cannot have that on top of everything else on my conscience. What say you, my friend?'

The Dalai Lama who had been observing everything and listening intently now sat forward his eyes bright and filled with knowing.

'I would say that he already is... is that not the truth, Jonas?'

I nodded imperceptibly.

'Very well!' said the Pope, 'then the least I can do is bless that rather large cross you wear around your neck, Jonas, for word has it, it is no ordinary cross, and I would make some recompense in the matter of your forefather, whom, it must be said possessed remarkable powers that I can only assume have been passed down to you?'

Again I nodded.

'Then come, let me make peace with all that you are and all that he was, and know that I will pray for the soul of he who was known as Simon the Sorcerer and ask for forgiveness...' he smiled and I removed the cross from around my neck.

'I, too, would like to add my blessing, if I may' said the Dalai Lama, and I watched as these two great men sealed our pact as they added their protection to the only thing in the world that would keep me safe from the Devil and knew what it felt to be truly humbled.

Chapter 13

  By evening I was safely ensconced within the opulent confines of the Vatican, and one of the first things I did was to call Menna with the news. She was as excited at this new development as she was eager to visit.
'I miss you, cariad,' she said, 'it seems so long since I saw you.'
I steeled myself, for there would be an unknown stretch of time before us yet and as privileged as my status had suddenly become, even the Pope would draw the line at unmarried female guests!
'I will come home as soon as I am able, but it won't be for some time yet, Menna, I have been granted a special pass that will allow me to access to some of the world's most rare and religious writings for there is still much study before me and well...you know my situation.'
Menna's laugh tinkled down the phone and I realised that I too, was missing her more than I cared to admit, but I may never get another chance to be in this unique position and so I pushed the feelings down.
'Know your situation?' she mocked playfully, 'Oh Jonas, I don't even know the half, but hey-ho, everything has it's time and place. Just don't go falling in love with some raven-haired beauty!'
'What? How could I, when I have a Titian-haired beauty waiting for me at home!'
As we laughed and joked together it was a welcome distraction from the endless questions and examining I had been subjected to over the past few days and we ended the call on a high note that came crashing down as I saw Einion suddenly appear in the doorway of the small study where I was sitting.
'Einion, what is it?' I said as I replaced the phone into its receiver.
'And why are your cases with you?'
'There is a late night flight back to Manchester and if it's all the same to you I would like to be on it,' he said simply.
'What? Why?'
'Because my work here is done; I have delivered you safely and now it's time to go home. Besides, the *hiraeth* is strong upon me, Jonas,

and all of this pomp and splendour is beyond me,' He lifted his shoulders, 'I am a plain and simple God-fearing man who feels like a fish out of water. I need to go home, have a decent *panad* eat food that doesn't contain olive oil and tomatoes and feel the Welsh mist soft on my face.'
I swallowed. I had not been expecting this. Einion had been a big part of life for the past two years and now he was going!
'Would you consider staying just a few more days? I've got used to having you around, and who on earth am I going to speak Welsh with now if you go!' I kept my tone light but there was a quiet determination in his face.
'No, Jonas, I'm afraid not, my friend. I need to remove myself from this whole environment; it is simply just too much for me. I have already explained my feelings to the Bishop and he has agreed I may return home.'
Something occurred to me then and I sobered suddenly.
'Einion, has this something to do with what happened today?'
By that I meant my stint of levitating. I recalled his gasp of shock...dismay? Had it all simply been too much for him?
He raised his shoulders imperceptibly and averted his eyes and therein was the answer. He had been an honest and steady companion and I respected him immensely. I had no wish to compromise his innate sense of integrity by forcing him to lie.
'I will miss you.'
'I will miss you, too. It has been ... an interesting journey and one I'm not likely to forget in a hurry,' he murmured and there were tears in his eyes, 'but you'll come along and say hello the next time you're in Bangor, won't you?'
I looked at him intently and knew then in that moment that it really had all become too much for him and my heart ached for this plain stolid man who lived only for his books and rising swiftly I went to him and held out my hand.
For the first time in two years he looked at my hand if he thought it would bite him which reaffirmed what I already knew in my heart. He was frightened of me.
'Mae'n iawn, Einion,' I said softly in Welsh, and watched as he tentatively took my hand as though we were strangers and my heart

ached anew.

'I will never forget all that you have done for me. Thank you, Einion, thank you, for *everything*...'

We gazed at each other in silence for some moments, remembering all of the talks, the debates, the lessons in class, and now we would part ways forever; I knew this as surely as I knew that my submergence into a more mystical world was so far beyond his ken as to be unbearable, and that whenever I returned to visit my adopted land it would perhaps be a kindness not to look him up.

'Pob lwc,' he said and I nodded.

A tap on the outer door heralded the entry of one of the palace servants.

'Would you like me to take your luggage down to the car, *monsieur?*' he enquired politely.

'Thank you,' said my old tutor and then relinquishing my hand, he gave me one final nod before hurrying after the porter.

I resumed my seat back behind the mahogany desk and thought about what had just happened and what it meant in terms of future relations between me and anyone who had full knowledge of who I was.

Something told me that this would be a common occurrence; people would come into my life, and people would go out, some perhaps, would stay and then there would be those who did not want to. Like Einion. I felt hurt and yet I understood,

It was a tall order to expect anyone without an exceptionally open mind to comprehend, never mind accept the truth of what I was, and that even those steeped in deep esoteric knowledge may well struggle as did one or two of the Pope's closest aides, whose fear and uncertainty I had felt during my interview.

It was a sobering thought and one I had not really considered before. Being somewhat of an introverted nature, closeted by years of study that had been relieved with trips back home, excursions with the twins, not to mention our time in Africa, and my next thought was of Menna.

Would she be able to handle it? Would she even wait! What were the chances of long-distance love surviving and would she want to be with me anyway once she knew the truth?

Einion's swift departure had made me think in a way that not even the thinly veiled disapproval of my family had not, but I was young still and headstrong and I loved Menna and if she was determined to wait, then I would be there at the other end. But I vowed there and then that I would be truthful with her when the time came, and allow her the ultimate decision.

Another tap at the door drew my attention. It was one of the aides who I had met during the earlier visits. There was no change in the friendliness of his manner so I assumed he hadn't yet been informed of today's events.

'Ah, Jonas, we thought you would be lonely on your first night, especially as your colleague has decided to leave so suddenly, so we have arranged a small supper in your honour. I'm hoping that this is agreeable to you.

In my honour!

Inwardly I smiled. I had just gone from losing someone whose affection for me had been replaced by fear, to an invitation for a private supper in my honour. The irony was not lost upon me but I accepted gracefully, for I was alone now in a strange and alien world and I would need to proceed cautiously, mindful that not everyone would be accepting, careful not to cause offence.

I was right to err on the side of caution as it soon became apparent that there were several within the Pope's inner circle who could not, or refused, to accept my unique status, and although they were careful to keep these feelings hidden, I picked up on the vibe nevertheless. That I was unusual, I knew. Tall, black-skinned, and with a strong Welsh accent that would set heads spinning whenever I opened my mouth. And then there were my tattoos, of course, an intricate design on each cheek that curved up to my eyebrows. But they were the mark of my calling, and as many would look and stare openly I was never aware of them, for I had absorbed them and their meaning into me as you would the rays of the sun. They were a part of me. They were my protection and my essence; they were the mark of God.

The days went by and then the weeks as I submerged myself into studies of a more esoteric nature as the private and less frequented realms of the Vatican library was opened up to me.

I saw scrolls and tomes so ancient, they had not seen the light of day for over a millennia and profound writings of sects long gone, and like a sponge I absorbed it all as my mind widened and became more attuned in greater understanding.

There were such mysteries of which I could never speak; whole volumes of *majick* and scriptures written by long-forgotten hands that had once held holy ones and testimonies of people who had witnessed miraculous acts and beheld beings so strange there were no names for them.

I pored over lost scrolls and ancient texts that hinted of otherworldly things; but I could find nothing of my ancestor, the man they called Simon the Magician. It was as though he had never existed.

But my search wasn't wholly in the pursuit of my controversial and infamous ancestor; there was study to be made of deep spiritual matters that went beyond the call of Christian conformity.

And I wasn't disappointed.

I had been sworn to the utmost secrecy, however; that anything discovered that may be at variance with the teachings of the church would not be divulged under *any* circumstances! There had been documents to sign and solemn oaths given to ensure my complete discretion, and aware of how reluctantly permission had been granted by those in charge of the inner sanctum, I gravely complied knowing also, that it was His Holiness who had had the final say and his open-mindedness was commendable.

Menna kept me abreast of events at home, as did my family with frequent phone calls, emails and letters, and that link with the world I'd once known seemed as far away as Ethiopia and sometimes I'd catch myself thinking of mountains and deserts and rain; for I had the *hiraeth* for both places, so when Menna said she'd be flying out for a week I greeted the news with pleasure.

'I can't wait to see you any longer, Jonas!' she'd announced, 'It's been far too long, so I've taken the initiative and booked a flight!' Typical Menna! Impulsive, resourceful, ever her own woman and I couldn't wait to see her. She had finished University and was currently working at the campus library. It would do me good to come out from such an intense period of study and I was keen to show her the sights.

To avoid courting disapproval Menna had wisely chosen a small guesthouse just off *Campo de' Fiori,* a bustling tourist area that had once been the site of public executions. A rather grim reminder was the statue of a man called Giordano Bruno, a free-thinking philosopher whose beliefs saw him burnt at the stake. It was with no small amount of irony that his writings which had been confiscated by the Holy Office were now buried deep within the Vatican archives under *The Index of Forbidden Books,* and I made a mental note to seek them out at the first opportunity.

But first there was Menna; vibrant, vivacious, my beautiful Menna! For the few days we were together, I dispensed with my usual clerical garb and donned jeans and more casual wear. After some inner debate I also decided to leave my staff behind. I still stood out, but Rome was so cosmopolitan with tourists I was, for a short time, nothing more than an exceptionally tall black sightseer and a bright-eyed lover. Rome was full of them. But as tempting as it was, I refrained from consummating our relationship, as much out of respect for Menna as it was for the gravity of my position. I dared not.
That I loved her and wanted to be with her was not in doubt, and already I had decided that I wanted to marry her – if she would have me. But if I was to be able to protect her and keep her safe, there was much I needed to do first.
It was clear that her feelings were mutual as she clasped me in a fierce hug.
'Oh Jonas, *bach*, how I've *missed you!'*
It has become her pet name for me, *Little* Jonas, and despite this obvious inaccuracy I loved her all the more for it and with equal fervour hugged her back.
'Why Jonas,' she cried laughingly, 'if you grow any taller I will need a ladder! *Iesu Grist* what are they feeding you?'
It was so good to see her and we caught up amidst endless cups of coffee in between walking hand in hand as we took in the sights. It was inevitable, of course, and it wasn't as though I hadn't been warned. I had been aware of them on various forays out from the Vatican but I hadn't expected them to come at me so soon or so boldly. I'm talking about the *shetani* low level spirit forms that could wreak havoc if allowed.

But their influence was limited and like that time with my encounter with the baboon, I knew I could handle myself and besides, I was older now, bigger, taller and adept in all manner of fighting arts; which was why they came at me *enmasse*.

It was Menna's last night and as had been my wont, I had left the staff safely back in my quarters. My height and colour drew enough attention as it was without any further accruements, religious or otherwise, and caught up in the pleasure of being reunited with Menna, therein I made my first mistake for they had obviously been waiting and biding their time, and foolishly I gave it to them on a plate.

Chapter 14

Everyone has that sixth sense, that hidden eye, but for many it remains a blind spot, a suppressed awareness, conscious or otherwise. Some are born with it, attuned and wide-open; others dig deep to cultivate it, and then there are those who will never know the fortuity of having such a gift. For my part, being in possession of such a precious God-given commodity undoubtedly saved our lives that day, but the experience shook me to the core and I vowed never to go abroad again without proper protection.

People are naturally curious, and as my appearance often pulled eyes in my direction I had become accustomed to stares and muttered remarks, and yet there is another kind of regard that is akin to a chill wind and you know it when you feel it, for it carries with it the unmistakable message of *danger* - and you ignore it at your peril. During the rare visits when I'd left the Vatican for one reason or another, I had become aware on occasion of being under scrutiny and would cast about before my eyes would alight upon someone stood back from the crowd with a stillness about them that would mark them out.

As an individual they were nondescript to any casual observer, just another face in the crowd, but I would sense the intensity in their gaze and would deliberately pause to return the stare until they slipped away like thieves in the night.

My presence in Rome had not gone undetected, but as yet it was merely the curiosity of lower caste spirits and I was not duly worried. Until that night.

Menna and I had been out for a dinner at a small bistro and were making our way back through the winding streets when I had the uncanny but indisputable sense that we were being followed.

Not wanting to spook Menna unnecessarily I glanced back a couple of times only to see no one in sight, but there was a prickling throughout my body and I knew were in danger.

There was still some way to the hotel, dusk was falling and something told me to change direction and quickly. Without so much of a word I pulled Menna in front of me into a narrow alley.

'Wha...what? What are you *doing*, Jonas!'

'Keep moving, Menna, just keep moving!'

She did as she was bid but with a muffled curse and soon we found ourselves in a small square with more alleys leading off. Swiftly I went towards the furthest one as Menna whispered.

'What's going on, Jonas, what's happening?'

'Something is following us, try not to panic, just stay close.'

'Something!'

'Someone but more than one, now hush, Menna, this way!'

We came out onto a long street and once again I pulled us into another alley, but it was futile, of course, for by the time we emerged into another square they were already there waiting for us and soft footfalls behind us told me we were trapped.

I stepped easily to the side and drew Menna behind me.

Her breathing was the only sound I took in the sight of the men stood before us.

They stared back in silence and somewhere in the distance a dog set up a howl.

The square was small and deserted. Shutters were closed on the buildings and doors remained shut as the last of the light faded away and a pale moon rose

I took in my adversaries. There were five of them, including our light-footed pursuer who now eased from the alley to go and stand besides his associates. There was something familiar about each and every one of them and I knew I had seen their ilk before.

Slightly scruffy and with sallow looks, they had an air of quiet desperation about them, more commonly found among those whose solace could only be found through drugs. Easy pickings for the ever-opportunist *shetani,* and the latter had been unusually clever by forming a group.

Lower caste spirits were known to usually work alone and seeing them come together like this was as disconcerting as it was unexpected.

Steel glinted in the hands of all of them as their eyes flicked between me and Menna with a wolfish intent.

Menna.

Was that their plan? They knew they would have a job to take me, but Menna ...

It was our last night before she returned home and something told me that they knew this. And so distracted had I been, no doubt they'd been following us about all week which was why I recognised their faces. I had seen them and they'd been noted, but only on the most peripheral level.

In that moment Samuel's warnings came back to haunt me, but now wasn't the time to reflect on my stupidity.

There was only way to deal with this and I had to move fast. Before they knew what was happening I was suddenly amongst them and let loose every honed move I had ever mastered since I'd been taught how to fight. Desperation drove me as their soft bodies gave way before my flurry of blows. I had taken them by surprise but not for long.

They rallied and came at me with renewed vigour, their eyes maniacal, their movements clumsy, but it was the glints of metal were the greater danger as they jabbed and slashed towards me looking for an opening.

'*Jonas!*'

Menna's shriek was full of fear and for the first time in my life I felt a rising fury that all but threatened to overwhelm me. It was almost primeval and fuelled by my determination to protect at all costs but it clouded my focus and I felt a sharp sting on my wrist and another on my thigh.

'Jonas!' shouted Menna again and then like a cool breeze through my mind I felt something touch me and the rage subsided as clarity returned.

These were *shetani*; nothing more, nothing less. Just low life spirits that fed on the weakness of others. I was more than a match for them. Almost serenely I harnessed my energy and became little more than a powerful weapon as I kicked and parried, slashed and fought until the last assailant fled moaning into the night.

Lights had now come on in some of the houses but no one ventured outside into the square. Menna rushed across and grabbing at me cried, 'Oh you're bleeding!'

'Nothing much, just scratches. Are you alright, Menna?'

'*Me!*' Her tone was indignant. 'Jonas, you've just fought off *five* men and you ask if I'm alright! *Iesu Grist!*'

'I'm fine, just slightly winded.' I glanced about but the square remained deserted except for unseen eyes. 'Come on, let's get you back to the hotel.'

'And you back to the Vatican I think! Is it safe for you to go out?' Menna was on the verge of tears and I hugged her to me fiercely.

'Yes, of course, we were just unlucky.'

I remained vigilant as we made our way back through the streets but there was no sign of my assailants. They were long gone and I inwardly cursed my carelessness.

It could never happen again.

'But what did they want? Why were they following us?'

'They were looking for no good, Menna; let's just leave it at that. The world is full of thieves and muggers, we just happened to be in the wrong place at the wrong time. Now cease your fretting, look we're here.'

In her room Menna made hot, sweet tea for both of us from the hospitality tray. A small orange lamp glowed in the corner as we sat on the bed in silence. Menna had insisted on inspecting my wounds as soon as we got in, but they were nothing more than shallow cuts, and after cleaning them thoroughly they now ached dully beneath a couple of plasters courtesy of the hotel manager.

'They were not muggers, not in the real sense ... were they, Jonas.' Menna said eventually, 'This I know as I also know that there is something about you, that you are different, yes! But *how* different? I need to know. Truth now, cariad.'

I rose and went to stand by the window. It looked out over a cluster of buildings that loomed darkly against the night sky and I knew in my heart that the moment had come.

'You're right, I am different, but it is not as straightforward as you think. I have a calling quite like no other, and it will be as much a bane of my life as it will be a blessing, for it marks me out in many ways, but I had not expected anything like this – not so blatantly.'

'*An attack?*' Menna echoed. 'Jonas they had *knives,* they were going to kill you! And yet you speak of it as though it was a mere skirmish in the park!' She shook her head in disbelief, 'Jonas, you could have been *killed!*'

It was typical of Menna that she should think of others before herself and seeing the concern in her face I felt a flush of shame. That I had ever thought myself worthy of such selfless and all-consuming love, and yet here it was – and from the very woman whose life I'd risked.

'Menna, I cannot apologise enough for having put you in so much danger,' I said quietly, 'For your life is more precious than my own, and I am furious at myself for having put you in such a position. I am *so* sorry, *cariad*...'

'You couldn't have known! You were not to know! But after what I saw tonight I have no doubt that there are greater things at work around you which is why you are a target for these...*dark forces*. And although I may not believe in the devil in the conventional sense, I believe in the power of evil...but more importantly, I believe in *you!*'

I stared at her for a moment, I had never seen her so impassioned which made what I was about to say more difficult.

As though in anticipation of this she rose came swiftly to stand before me and took my hands in hers.

'I trust you, Jonas. I would trust you with my life and don't even think about trying to call it a day, because I won't have it, I'm telling you. Whatever it is you do, or are expected to do, I intend to be right by your side, and besides,' she made a small puffing noise a defiant light in the hazel eyes, 'it would take more than a few skinny men with questionable body hygiene to put me off! And oh, how you saw them off, Jonas, *Iesu Grist,* they didn't know what hit them! How did you learn to fight like that? I knew you'd done Karate or something but ...'

'Menna,' I began and she put a finger to my lips.

'No, Jonas, I mean it. You know better than anyone that I'm not a quitter, and I'm certainly not going anywhere, and if you try to force the issue ...' the defiant light in her eyes was replaced by a mischievous one, 'I'll beat down the door to the Vatican myself and give that Pope of yours a piece of my mind, then you'll really be in trouble!'

I laughed in spite of myself and hugged her to me.

'Ah, how I love to hear you laugh, Jonas, you're always usually so serious but what a special man you are, and you're *my* man, and don't you forget it!'.

'Oh Menna, my Menna, you don't know the half, and this probably isn't a one-off attack. No doubt there will be more, only from where and from what I have no idea. But what I do know is that to be with me is a huge risk, I see that now.'

'Life is full of risks, Jonas. And why should we deny ourselves the chance to be together,' She drew back and looked up at me searchingly, 'It's what you want, isn't it?'

'You know it is, it's just ...'

'Just what?'

Something stirred deep within me, like the reverberation of a distant echo and I pushed it away.

'It will not be easy. Life with me will not be easy. There will be dangers and uncertainties and times when you will have to listen to me, even when your head may say otherwise.'

She raised an eyebrow.

'And this is what worries me! You are strong-willed, Menna, and as much as I love that quality in you, I will never know when you might take it upon yourself to do the opposite and if something happened, I could not bear it.'

'Then I will make a vow.'

'What?'

She grinned up at me.

'Well, what's good for the goose is good for the gander, and it's not as though you haven't had to make a few in your time, is it? I will make an oath and I will do it now.' She went across to the bedside unit and opened the top drawer before coming back to stand before me a small bible in her hands.

'Well?'

'Menna, it's not that simple...'

'What? Do you doubt the word of God now, Jonas? You know how I feel about the whole religious thing, but if this is what it takes then I'll swear on this bible now and gladly!'

We gazed at each other in silence for some moments as I struggled to find the right words. Menna had a set look but a deeper emotion was threatening that belied the brave front, and in the face of such

determination I capitulated.
Covering her hands and the bible with mine I raised them to my lips before saying, 'No, it is I who will make a vow and that I will always love you and keep you safe, that you shall be as my right hand and that once my time here is over you will be forever by my side...but only on one condition.'
'Name it,' breathed Menna her eyes bright with unshed tears.
'That until my studies are over, you remain in Wales and I will come to you. It will be safer there and I will have peace of mind knowing that whatever waits for an opportunity, it will stay close to where I am and not you. Do you understand what it is I'm saying, Menna?'
She nodded and her chin began to tremble.
'Then let us take an oath together, that whatever comes in the future we will face it together and may God watch over you, *cariad*. For there is no telling where this journey will take us, but know that your trust will be tested, Menna, as will be everything you thought you ever knew and so if you're sure this is what you really want.'
She gazed up at me with such trust I never loved her more than I did in that moment, and as a warning went off deep within me, I ignored it nevertheless, for what man could deny a woman who wanted to give of herself so utterly.
I watched as she drew my hands slowly towards her mouth, and I felt her kiss like a fragile feather as still holding my gaze she made her vow and there we sealed our love as I went down on one knee as Rome slept around us.

Chapter 15

  Our news was greeted with no great surprise by our families, but I sensed disquiet, nevertheless and chose to ignore it. We were both adults, we were deeply in love, and it was our decision. We were careful, however, never to mention what had happened that night in the belief that such a revelation would only hinder our determination to be together.
The months flew past as I buried myself ever deeper in the archives of esoteric knowledge before finally receiving the formal invitation from the Israeli Ministry of Interior I'd been waiting for.
Not all Jews of Ethiopian descent were welcome in the Holy Land, but the uniqueness of my station, sanctioned by the Vatican itself, secretly, ensured that curiosity won out in the end and I was summoned to appear before the Chief Rabbis.
I am often asked what denomination I follow; and my answer is always the same; God's.
My refusal to be drawn further into religious argument has always been the one thing that tantalises and frustrates, but it is my only protection against an ever-growing sea of diverse and different thought and so I keep the peace by keeping mine.
It was almost with a sense of relief when I left Rome for the next part of my journey. Having started my life in the dustbowl of a desert, to then spend my formative years in a comfortable but modest cottage, to be immersed in the opulence of His Holiness's abode could often feel surreal and I would long for the simplicity of the cave up high in the Simian Mountains.
Security was tight at Israel's main airport, Ben Gurion, and with my great cross round my neck and in my long black frock I drew the usual attention. Since the incident with Menna in the square, my sacred staff now never left my side. Knowing that it was easier to bypass unwanted attention by keeping it folded in its alternate form also allowed for smoother transition, because to all intents and purpose it was just a wooden cross, albeit a large one

Israeli security eyed me closely as I passed through the various checkpoints, and at the final point I was met by a serious-faced man who introduced himself as Elam Mahmid, representative of The Chief Rabbinate of Israel. As we shook hands the abruptness of his manner indicated to me that my visit was under sufferance and I felt grateful for the unwitting heads-up. Seemingly there would none of the stiff and yet courteous welcome I had experienced at the Vatican, and I braced myself accordingly.

The drive to Jerusalem was taken in a strange silence as my companion rode up front with the driver. Having been escorted to a black sedan as soon as we'd left the airport, I looked around me with interest as we sped along Highway 1 which was the main road from Tel Aviv, and inwardly I admitted to myself that it felt strange to find myself in the holiest of holy lands.

It was a scenic and unexpected journey, from the steep climb up to the Judean mountains where you were greeted by a museum of old military vehicles left as a testament to Israel's fight for independence, before the road curved down before ascending once again as it saved the best for last; a sharp turn and then the most spectacular view as the road swept down the infamous Motza Curve.

I drew breath as the driver expertly took the bend as Elam Mahmid turned briefly and gave me a tight smile, and then we were climbing steadily towards the ancient city of Jerusalem as the road wound as though drawing us in, and then soon we were through the tunnels and into the city proper.

'We are taking you directly to the Beit Yahav building, that is, if you are not too tired after your journey, Rev ... er ... Llewellyn.'

He struggled just slightly with the pronunciation of my second name, as many people did, but I detected a hint of insolence in his tone and gave him a measured look. The fact I was being taken directly to The Chief Rabbiate of Israel was not lost upon me; either the church officials were extremely keen to meet me, or else I was being quite succinctly put in my place.

'Not at all, although a chance to freshen up would be welcome before my meeting, perhaps...'

'Of course,' was the reply and then we were off the street as the car swept down to an underground area where security waited before waving us through.

Once inside the building I was shown to a rest-room as someone else took my luggage for safe-keeping. After freshening up I regarded myself for some moments in the mirror as I searched for signs of nervousness and saw none.

They would be banking on that, I knew, and I felt akin how Daniel must've felt before being thrown to the lions and unlike Daniel, I had more than my faith and the knowledge of this would sustain me. Such self-assurance gave me an edge and a confidence way beyond my years, and this did not sit well with those of mature and equally self-assured standing. The religious leaders here were renowned for their propensity to fierce debate, and so I braced myself for what I knew would not be an easy meeting.

I was not disappointed.

Upon being ushered into a large brightly-lit room, there were sat before me a row of bearded, gimlet-eyed officials who ceased talking as I entered the room, and there fell a silence so sudden you could have heard a pin drop.

Two large well-built men rose from where they sat at the centre of the long table and held out their hands as one said, 'Forgive us, a most unsettling welcome, I'm sure. We are the Chief Rabbi; please, step forward, Reverend so we can make the necessary introductions.'

I did as I was bid, as one after another the rest of the company stood up and shook my hands. I counted twelve in total but doubted I would remember half of the names.

They all looked uncannily familiar and yet different; some wore glasses, several the customary ringlets, but all, without exception, wore the 'kippah', the small traditional; skull-cap and with it a look of keen interest as I took my seat before them.

I sipped at the water as Chief Rabbi Abadi, the elder of the two shuffled some papers before them.

'You have come before us, Mr Llewellyn, with the most extraordinary claims. And yet we must give them out utmost attention on the understanding that we neither believe, nor disbelieve at this point, and that there are questions we must ask of you in the most...rigorous of terms.'

The speaker was the more thick-set of the two chief rabbi's who had a dark lustrous beard that he now smoothed thoughtfully with a well-manicured hand.

'I am ready and willing to answer all questions set out before me – within reason,' I replied and saw a sea of eyebrows lift in surprise and I suppressed a smile. 'But there are some things that I am afraid remain between me and God, but I will be happy to demonstrate the sanctioning of his power in other ways.'

That threw them and there then ensued a cacophony of indignant whispering before the second Chief Rabbi, Reb Ester called the company to order, and fixing me with a stern look he said.

'Mr Llewellyn, you are here at our invitation and may I remind you at your initial request. Therefore, to address my learned brethren with such an obtuse statement warrants no small concern. And we would have you comprehend that by claiming kinship to a man of dubious regard, we are, quite rightly, intent upon investigating this assertion further with the view you will prove nothing less than cooperative in pursuit of the truth.'

There were nods and grunts in reply to this as inwardly I took a deep breath. It was not on the best foot with which to start, but if they thought I would go easily into the pit they were mistaken.

I smiled disarmingly.

'Sir, I assure you, as God is my witness that I have come before you with no other intention than to be open and honest, and as there are mysteries within the inner sanctum of your teachings that will never be revealed; so there is with mine...' I spread my hands, 'I seek only to add to my knowledge with a greater understanding, and with nothing less than the greatest of respect.'

There was silence for some moments as my words sank in and then clearing his throat, the first Rabbi said, 'Very well. Let us proceed, as it were, for we have much to get through and as this is a preliminary hearing let us touch on the main points for now; Mr Llewellyn has come of his own volition after all, and is to all intents and purposes still a guest.'

A few in the company bristled at that, including the second Rabbi, but heads nodded, albeit reluctantly and I felt some of the tension leave the room.

'Mr Llewellyn, I would like to ask about your alleged kinship to the man they called Simon Magus. It is an incredible claim, it has to be said, for little is known about him other than as he came as mysteriously as he disappeared - but not before he caused much controversy and yet you claim direct descent from this man?'
'Yes, I do indeed, Sir.'
Chief Rabbi Ester leaned forward.
'So what evidence do you have to support this claim, other than the word of your family who, by your own admission, neither abide by nor practice any form of Semitic religion? And yet you also claim kinship to one of the Lost Tribes – how can this be?'
'By the word of God, Sir.'
Again all eyebrows shot up.
'Then, how...what...'
'In the usual way, Sir, there is no great mystery.'
There rose a slight rumbling at my remark and the two rabbi's waved for silence.
'Mr Llewellyn, there will always be great mystery around the will of *Yahweh*, and for all our learned lore more fool is he who would even think to countenance it. It is blasphemy of the highest level and an affront in the eyes of God!'
'Sir, you misunderstand me, I meant by word of prayer and contemplation.'
The tension was back. More intense this time as every man in the room eyed me with open hostility.
'He speaks no differently to me as he does to any of you,' I went on, 'But then as I can only bear witness to myself with any real certainty, that is, perhaps, a more appropriate statement, and as he is also my witness, may he strike me down if I speak nothing but the truth as I know it.'
Mt stance was unpalatable to them, I knew. For here was I not yet twenty and yet holding my own against a room full of elders with nothing more than quiet self-assertion in the face of their disbelief. They were not used to this. A boy, and an upstart no doubt in their eyes, unbowed in their presence and radiating such self-assurance it was all but unprecedented. But I could not allow the differences of our station detract me from the purpose of my visit, as I would not be

browbeaten into a religious box.

An explosion of sound came from the far end of the table as a grey-bearded individual guffawed loudly.

'*What?* Are you going to claim direct descent from the holy mother now as well as the false apostle! And what's that going on with your face? What does it mean - and what man of God would even *think* to bear such marks?'

I smiled in spite of myself as he let out an indignant huff that was echoed by others.

The Chief Rabbi's raised his hands and appealed for decorum, but I was unfazed. Such resistance was to be expected. Indeed I'd have been seriously concerned if I had not. But I had done my homework and had come prepared. It was simply a matter of appeasing the Rabbiate enough for them to allow me access to study with the ultimate aim of full acceptance.

They had secrets libraries of their own, I knew, and as my bloodline, arguably or not, came directly from one of the Ten Tribes of Israel, there was an unspoken right that hovered over us like a persistent ghost and they knew it. Samples of my blood had already been sent ahead for analysis and there was no disputing the findings.

I folded my hands into my lap and waited.

'Jonas ... can I call you Jonas?' Rabbi Ester turned to me his manner earnest fatherly almost. 'We are at great pains to make of this meeting the best that we can do, and so you must forgive Rabbi Abrams for his outburst, but we are all struggling to comprehend as to where this is leading and we need more than fine words and arguments. So perhaps you would care to begin with a demonstration of your powers?'

I was being patronised and without the benefit of any form of subtlety and I felt the first flush of anger since coming into the room. I lowered my eyes so that they could not see the fire in them and in calm modulated tones began to speak.

'Fine words perhaps, but ones not so easily dismissed when directed through spirit, so I hope you will not be too disappointed. I have no written words, as you know, with which to show you the validity of my claim, but I do have what knowledge of another kind, and so as a courtesy, Rab Ester, I thought I would begin with you.'

I closed my eyes and opened up and it was as though a warmth air blew through me and then came the information; fluid and strong.
'I would tell you that the estrangement of your brother will be resolved once you release to him the documents he seeks; they are to all intents and purposes right fully his, and that should you do so by the date he has indicated there will be no need for further action.'
Rabbi Ester made a strangled noise in the back of his throat and I paused respectfully as he glared at me thunderously.
'*What!* What game is this you are playing, young man? And let me tell you, as God is *my* witness that nobody, *not one soul* outside of my family knows of this! And so who is your source? For I will have him, I'm telling you and you'll not leave this room until *I do!*'
I looked up at him mildly and his face was the colour of puce. The brethren had drawn back and were gazing at each other in muted bewilderment and spreading my hands I said simply, 'Why Sir, and with all due respect, you already *have* him, for it is God himself, and he abides with us...but then far be it from me to remind you of that.'
The Chief Rabbi gaped at me and I held his stare calmly until he made a concerted effort to calm down. The silence in the room was deafening. No one moved and somewhere out in the street a car horn blared,
'What more have you ... does ... *He*, have to say on this matter?' said Reb Ester tightly. Some colour had returned to his cheeks but he was struggling to contain himself, I knew.
'Only that your father rues this dispute between you and urges reconciliation, as he did during the last moments of his life.'
As the Rabbi stared at me transfixed I then looked to his counterpart and gave a small nod.
'Rabbi Abadi, you are waiting on tests for testicular cancer and have hardly slept these past few nights. The good Lord bids you cease in your worrying for the results will be in this very day and the news will be good.' I smiled at his shocked bewilderment and then turned to the next and then the next, as I imparted information so singularly personal, each disclosure left gasps in my wake before finally I came to the elder who had mocked me earlier.
 He all but flinched as I laid my eyes upon him, and I raised a hand reassuringly.

'Sir, please, let there be ill-feeling between us for I speak only that have been given by God himself so that you,' my gaze swept the company, 'all of you ... understand that I come in peace, in *his* name and for learned reasons only. The purpose of these revelations is not to cause shame or embarrassment, but to prove beyond doubt, that I am blessed with God's truth and the power of his mysticism and that this is at his behest and his alone.'
I turned back to the old greybeard who now regarded me with a new respect and I bowed my head.
'Sir, I have deliberately left you until last because the good Lord has an extra special message for you.'
I paused and all heads now craned to look at the recipient of the last message.
'He would have you know that all the answers of which you seek shall be yours when you enter the Kingdom of Heaven. There your wife awaits you, as does your child,' my voice became gentle as tears bloomed in the old man's eyes, 'I believe you named her Rachel, for your mother. She too, waits for you there.'
The final testimony given I leaned back in my chair and closed my eyes feeling suddenly very tired.
A polite cough roused me and I looked up to meet the gaze of Rabbi Ester who now slowly rose and extended a hand.
'We need no more from you this day, young man, other than an assurance that you'd be willing to come back before us, only to a more receptive committee and of that, I can promise you.'
I stood up and gave his hand a firm shake as Rabbi Abadi followed suit his eyes still bearing the look of a stunned animal.
'There is only one way you could have known all those things,' he breathed, 'I have sat here and listened and as God is my witness, there is only one way...'
He clasped both of my hands and murmured a blessing as one by one each man in the room rose and gathered around. I felt their constraints fall away as an ice cap melts before the sun as each one shook my hand. It was a poignant moment and worth the initial hostility.
'We have much to discuss and you are no doubt desperate for some much-needed rest,' said Rabbi Ester, 'and what hosts would we be to deny you all comforts at our disposal? And so follow me, if you will,

for I have a car waiting and we will repair until the morrow, God willing, we have not offended you too much.'

I offered him a warm smile.

'Sir, there has been no offence committed that I am aware of, other than a genuine need to seek the truth, and for that I am most grateful. We are all God's children after all, and if we are to commune and work with each other, then there can be no other way than by acceptance of each other. And so count me in for this meeting tomorrow, and perhaps the good Lord will reveal more of what are unequivocally his mystical talents. I am merely the instrument, remember. But I am pleased, nevertheless, that my tune finally appealed to you.'

I looked with pointed humour at the elder Rabbi and he smiled back toothlessly his eyes bright. And from that moment began the first of many secret and often animated meetings with the Rabbiate as they finally embraced me as one of their own and gave leave for me to study their ancient texts.

In the months that followed I made two trips back home to the excited welcome of my family and the fervent embraces of Menna. They wanted to know everything, of course, the holy land held a fascination for many, but I would not be drawn other to say that I was enjoying the extended study and that I hoped to be back in Wales soon.

God had other ideas, however, when some weeks later I received a call from Samuel.

He has travelled all the way into Gondar to have use of a phone, and when he spoke to my parents he refused to impart the news to anyone else but me personally.

Hearing his voice across the miles was strange, but what he had to tell me was stranger still.

Even after I had replaced the receiver my mind struggled to comprehend what it was he had just told me. The implications were massive; the impact, if it was true, would be nothing less than cataclysmic.

He believed he had found my father and that he was *alive!*

Chapter 16

I could say nothing to anyone, of course. The news came like a thunderbolt and in something of a daze I made the necessary arrangements. Usually calm and collected, I could feel my heart racing as I made my excuses to the Rabbiate that I'd been called away on family business and would have to leave immediately.
Rabbi Abadi eyed me keenly.
'Will you be coming back?'
'I don't know. But I will be in touch.'
He laid a hand on my arm.
'Jonas, are you quite alright? You seem upset ... is there anything we can do?'
I shook my head.
'No, thank you for your concern, Rabbi, but this is strictly family business.'
My sudden plan of action drew much speculation amongst the brethren, I knew, and I had become fond of each and every one of them. But I could not confide this recent development to even they, as I knew I could not to Menna, and it was then that we had our first argument.
'Why can't I come? What's this urgent business? And does your mother know? Perhaps I should ask her!'
'It would do no good, Menna, because she will be none the wiser. Just trust me please, that this is something I have to do alone.'
'Yes, but *what?*'
Her tone was demanding and I tried not to become irritated
'Menna ...'
'No, Jonas! I trust you, you know that, but what is so important that you have to go rushing off?'
I yearned to tell her. To be able to tell anyone! But I could not for fear of the impact it would cause. My mother, my half-siblings, their life and what it would mean for them. I had to get the facts first. I had to go out there and investigate further. Alone.
'I will tell you, I promise. Just not right now. Please, Menna, try to

understand that not everything I'm involved with is ... well, it's not always easy ...'

'There's no need to tell *me* that! I know, remember!'

A silence fell between us over the phone and I could tell by her breathing that she was trying not to cry.

'I'll not be away any longer than I have to, and then I promise I'll come straight back from Gondar. Just bear with me, please, Menna. I will make it up to you. I promise.'

'Promises, promises,' she muttered, 'as if I have a choice! And before you say anything, I know this is how it is. It just isn't always so easy for me either. I *miss* you, Jonas!'

'I know and I miss you, too,' My voice was gentle but I could feel the tension between us.

'Very well,' she said abruptly, 'just call me when you're ready to come home.'

As I replaced the receiver I simply had no idea when that would be; a week? A month?

It saddened me that Menna was so obviously hurt by my secrecy, but I knew little myself other than to make haste and that all would be revealed on my arrival.

Thankfully it was not a long flight, just a few hours, but long enough to think and wonder as my mind continued to churn about furiously.

I had prayed about it, of course, and reached out for a sense of what I was going into, but the veil was firmly down; I would literally have to wait and see.

As I alighted at Addis Ababa there was little time before the connecting flight to Gondar and I felt grateful for smoothness of my journey as I drew nearer to what could be the most pivotal point of my life.

My mother when I'd called to say I'd be making a trip had been no less avid than Menna, but I had dodged the barrage of questions for she knew by my tone that something big was afoot.

'Well whatever it is, just you be careful, Jonas, and don't go playing the hero – look what happened to your father!'

 I closed my eyes at the memory of those words spoken just hours before and full of innocent unknowing, and I could well imagine my

mother's reaction if I'd told her the truth. Not to mention Rhys; both would be shook to the core by the very notion, for where would they stand with their marriage!
And yet nothing was certain. Samuel only *thought* that he'd been found, but then knowing the usual unruffled nature of his mind, his barely-suppressed animation over the phone indicated to me that he was certain enough to summon me across from one continent to the other.
Since receiving the news I held a deep spasm within me like nothing I had ever experienced before. It was akin to the *frisson* of excitement that was held firmly in a taut grasp of anticipation, and I waved away all refreshment that had been placed before me for fear I wouldn't be able to keep it down.
I all but willed the plane to go faster and was the first to disembark as the heat hit me and I breathed in the hot air like a man seeking moisture.

Samuel was waiting just inside the greeting area and as we clasped hands I could see a whole host of emotions in his eyes and I could've wept!
'Jonas,' his voice had a shake in it I had not heard before and I drew him to me and gave him a hug.
'I am here, uncle, I am here. Come; let us get out of here. I want to know *everything*!'
Samuel led me to the usual car parking area, and as soon as we were on the road as my senses were assailed by the alien and yet familiar sights and sounds of this wild and beautiful country.
'So what do you know, but more importantly, *how?*'
I looked at Samuel closely for his manner was unusually reticent and I felt the first stirrings of apprehension.
He gave me a quick glance before returning his eyes to the road.
'Some days ago a stranger came to our village. He insisted that he speak with the elders. His appearance caused something of a stir, for he was by no means our usual kind of visitor, which made his story all the more remarkable. Upon hearing what he had to say, the elders sent for me immediately, and it soon became obvious that they were most distressed by what he had to say ...'

Samuel paused and drew a deep breath as I waited, my eyes riveted to his face.

'He said that your father had sent him. That he was near death and wanted to remove the last piece of the mystery before he died. His last and most earnest request was that we send for his son. *For you Jonas!* The stranger was most specific.'

A strange sensation came over me, like a slow burn and swallowing hard I said softly,

'Who was this man, this messenger, uncle? And what was it about him that caused such disquiet within the village?'

'Because he was from the Kunama people, Jonas, and far from home...'

I raised my eyebrows and waited.

'... home being Eritrea...' Samuel finished and this time I gasped.

'Eritrea!'

My uncle nodded and I looked out to the road ahead for some moments as my mind struggled to process this latest development. *Eritrea.* I mouthed the word as though tasting it as Samuel went on, his voice tight with emotion.

'We have had peace with our neighbours as you know since they gained their independence, and although there has been the occasional border skirmish, they have been far enough away as to have had no bearing, and so when this man walked into our village one day, well you can imagine our shock.'

'And this man, does he have a name?'

'Yes, he called himself Aman Emias. He'd travelled with two companions who had waited with their vehicle just outside the village. Of course we invited them in and ensured hospitality, but the nature of their business meant we could not tell the rest of the village, not as yet. Not until we know for sure.'

I gazed at him as I slowly shook my head.

'So when do we set out for Eritrea?'

Samuel nodded at the road.

'We already have. There is no time to waste. It will take us a few hours to get to the border but everything has been arranged for passage across. There are provisions in the back for the journey so take some sleep now if you can. All going well we should be at our

destination by late afternoon.'
It was almost too much to take in and happening so fast.
After believing my father had perished in the desert all those years ago I could not help but feel doubt as the incongruity of the situation as it revealed itself.
'How do you know? How do you know that what this man says is the truth? And why has it taken my father so long to make contact?'
My uncle gave me a level look.
'In answer to your first question; evidence was given in the form of a name. It was the secret name that we are all blessed with in the tribe. Aman would have had no way of knowing this, and that was proof enough for us all. As to the second question, only your father can tell us that. The message was simply that you go to him. The man Aman insisted that nothing more could be given than that. It was a dying man's wish, he said, and I merely the messenger.'
His voice cracked slightly at the end and I reached out and gave his shoulder a slight squeeze. This had also come as a huge shock to my uncle, for he, too had believed his brother lost all these years. With my mind I reached out fleetingly and could feel the turbulence of his emotions like a raging sea.

We drove on in silence for some minutes, each with our thoughts. Could it be true? Samuel seemed to think so and he was nobody's fool. I would've liked to have met this man Aman, to have questioned him for myself, and being inherently cautious I could not help but hold back the greater part of me that wanted to rejoice; for if life had taught me one thing hence far, was that not everything was as it seemed.
'I confess I am at a loss for words, uncle, but I trust your judgement enough to make this journey and God willing, it is my father who waits at the other end. But until then, tell me, what nature of man was the messenger Aman?'
'Gentle, unassuming ... we were all much taken with him as we were with his companions. All they would tell us was that they were from a small settlement just over the border and that your father had been with them many for years.'
It was as intriguing as it was highly unusual and as the car ate up the

miles we passed the Simien Mountains I gazed dreamily up at their peaks as inwardly I prayed for guidance.

'I understand your wariness in the face of this, Jonas,' Samuel offered after some time, 'for I would not have believed it myself had I not been first witness. But Aman was in earnest and true, there was no doubt of that. You will meet him when we reach the border for it will be he himself who will be escorting us across and directly to your father. Thank heavens you were able to come so quickly, for it had been made quite clear that we didn't have much time and for my part, I would travel the distance a thousand times over if it means looking on the face of my brother again!'

'Amen to that,' I murmured and reached into the back for some water.

'Here, uncle, you must drink,' I said unscrewing the top off a bottle and passing it to him, 'For if indeed my father lies waiting to make his peace, then there will be enough tears between us to fill the dead sea, I'm thinking.'

We looked at each other, hope shimmered like a living thing between us, and then we spoke no more as the hours crept past as the road took us nearer to honour the request of a dying man.

Chapter 17

I must have dozed off because hearing my name being called I opened my eyes to see that the light was fading and we had pulled off the road into the shade of some trees where two men were waiting.
'We are here, *Bekele*,'
I stretched and eased the crick in my neck as Samuel removed the keys before climbing out of his side of the car. I heard a murmur of voices and was instantly alert as two men dressed in white robes with a colourful wrap a-piece came forward and gave the customary greeting to my uncle who returned it in kind.
I exited the vehicle smoothly my eyes seeking the speakers before I was even out and I saw their faces lighten.
The smaller of the two stepped forward and gazed up at me as he nodded slowly.
'Yes, you are his son without doubt, and much like him. So tall, so strong,' he said gravely and then held out his hand, 'Hello Jonas, we meet at last. I am Aman of the Kunama people and this is my cousin Kidane. You have no idea how pleased we are to see you, but none will be more so than your father.'
I looked down into a round kindly face with a neatly-clipped beard and head full of hair. I had so many questions I didn't know where to start, but the first and most apt words that came out of my mouth were 'Thank you, thank you for this,' I shook his hand warmly.
Samuel stepped forward.
'Aman tells me the encampment is not too far from the border and that we must leave the car here and walk in.'
I became suddenly aware that I was still wearing my black cassock with the heavy wooden cross around my neck and turning back to Aman I said, 'Should I change, perhaps? I have more suitable clothing if you think this will draw unwanted attention.'
'There is no need, but perhaps in case we are spotted you could perhaps do something with the cross.'
I removed it from my neck and without fuss unfolded it into its alternative status of a staff. Aman looked on curiously before giving

a small nod.

'Before we go any further,' he said, 'I must tell you that you will not find your brother as you remember him,' He addressed this statement directly to my uncle whose face clouded with confusion.

'What do you mean?' he demanded sharply, 'And why did you not mention this before?'

Aman spread his hands in a gesture of appeasement.

'My apologies, Samuel, but I could say nothing without breaking an oath; your brother insisted. But know that the injuries he sustained were inflicted *before* he came to us. When we found him bleeding and close to death in the desert, we took him in and administered what healing we could, but ...' He threw me a rueful glance, 'he is not the man he was, but he has learned to live with his disabilities.'

Samuel and I stared at him for some moments lost for words.

I cleared my throat.

'What kind of disabilities?'

Aman laid a hand on his heart.

'You shall see. Please, let us move your vehicle further into the cover of the trees. There is much tension on these borders and we must take every precaution.'

I went to press further but he'd already turned away. His cousin bowed his head and followed him into the trees. I looked in quiet bewilderment to Samuel whose brow had furrowed like a pending storm.

'Peace, uncle,' I murmured softly, and he turned a tortured gaze upon me.

'What can he mean, Jonas ... *not the same man!* I feel my heart in my mouth and such a fear upon me at what we might find.'

I put my arm around him and drew him back to the car.

'We have come this far and we must trust a bit further for God is with us, and only He knows the reasoning to all of this. Come, uncle, they are waiting for us. Are you alright to drive?'

Samuel pulled away and rubbed at his temples.

'Yes, yes, I am alright, Jonas. It was just the shock. And you are right, *Bekele,* we have come this far on trust and needs be just a little more. But something pulls at the core of me like an unknown grief, and so perhaps we should both prepare ourselves for the worst, I'm thinking.'

He started the engine and I held my peace. I had nothing to add to that for I too, now bore the weight of a heavy heart. I watched as Samuel drove the car further into cover. Fortunately it was a dark colour and so merged easily into the dense foliage as Aman guided him in.

Satisfied that the car could not be seen from the road, our guide drew us all back together as the searing heat of the day started to give way to the night's chill.

Samuel had pulled our bags out from the car. It was only light luggage but it was wiser to leave nothing behind. He also took the water and a blanket that he drew around himself as Aman and his cousin helped take some of the load.

'Jonas, will you not take something warm to put on, here, take one of these blankets.'

'No, uncle, I am fine, but I will take the bags,' I replied in similar hushed tones.

'Once we leave the safety of the trees there must be no talking until we reach the encampment,' Aman instructed, 'Stay in single file and follow me.'

We set out as the dark hills loomed before us. Our guide picked his way unerringly along the uneven ground, he and Kidane nothing more than moving shapes and we knew we had crossed the border when he lifted his hand and stabbed with his finger.

The wail of a hyena came out over the distance, but Aman didn't pause and kept going forward until we were swallowed up in the recess darkness of the slopes that rose above us as the temperatures plunged and the sky filled with stars.

It was a most surreal moment among many I had experienced, tramping across alien territory to meet the man from whose loins I had sprung over twenty years before. I glanced to Samuel whose long legs easily kept pace, but whose head was lowered deep in thought. We were both at the mercy of unseen events and like him, I was trying to prepare myself for the worst.

By my reckoning we'd walked a mile or two before I became aware of dimmed firelight in the distance huddled deep within the hills and I gave my uncle a nudge.

He raised his head and then gave me a swift look before Aman called a halt and then turned to us smiling.

'Brothers, we have made it and safely, the good Lord be praised. We are nearly there, not far now.'

The pride and relief was evident in his voice and we were able to talk in low voices as the light of the fires grew brighter and then we could make out an array of tents and hustings that contained their livestock.

'Can we go straight to my brother? Will you take us directly there?'

Samuel's voice all but vibrated with emotion. In comparison I suddenly felt almost shy and unsure at the prospect of meeting this man who was to all intents and purposes, a stranger to me.

'Of course, he is waiting for you.'

A few dark figures were tending to the fires and watched us as we passed. I held on to my staff tightly as Aman led the way to a medium-sized tent where a faint light glowed from within. He pulled back the opening and stepped back.

The moment was here. A moment I had often wondered and dreamed about. *It was finally here!*

Inside was my father; my *natural* father, whose blood ran in my veins, and I felt a quietude come over me as my heartbeat slowed and my mind became calm. I glanced towards Samuel whose eyes were on me and he nodded.

I was to go first. As the first and only-born of this stranger within; it was I whom he had asked for, and it was I who would look upon him first. I drew a deep breath and stepped inside.

A long figure was lying on a pallet covered by blankets, and as my eyes struggled to adjust to the gloom there came a soft outtake of breath and then one word.

'Jonas.'

At the sound of my name my heart filled with love that only a child can know, and as though drawn by an invisible thread I suddenly found myself kneeling at the side of the bed.

As though in a dream I gazed into the face of the man who had once climbed mountains and strode the vast deserts, who had fought and suffered, loved and lost, and now, lying helpless like the fallen warrior he was, and despite all the ills that had been visited upon him, he smiled up at me with such unadulterated joy tears came to my eyes as I realised he had none.

Two sunken sockets were testament to what had befallen him that day so many years ago, and instinctively I reached down to clasp his hands only to find that in their place were two smooth stumps, and before I could stop it a groan of despair escaped me as I realised that these had been taken from him also.

'Father,' I cried, *'what did they do to you?'*

It was a moment of pure anguish and I could not help it so great was the shock. As tears rained down my face he reached up and brushed my cheek with as natural a movement as if his hands were still there, and in that moment, I felt his peace and it washed over me like a warm spring.

I quieted and we looked deeply at and into each other in a way that did not need the naked eye.

'My son,' he said softly, 'my only son ... how proud I am of you, and fear not, I see you, Jonas ... I see you well enough.'

I could not speak.

There were still traces of the handsome man my mother had fallen in love with, and I knew her heartbreak would know no bounds if she could see him now.

'How fares your mother... my beautiful Abeba?' he asked as though he had read my mind. 'She has found happiness in her new life I hope?'

I finally found my voice.

'Yes, she married a good man, you would like him, and he takes good care of her; he takes care of us all.'

It felt strange giving reassurance in this way but my answer seemed to please him as his face alighted with pleasure.

'Ah so you have siblings..? Then God has been kind and kept his promise ... and you, my son speak like music with an accent that is new to me ... yet it is pleasing in its sound. I like it much ...' He nodded slowly as though in private contemplation and I marvelled at the serenity of his being.

There was a long pause before a memory rose in my mind and almost shyly I asked the question.

'My mother told me once that you came to her in a dream. That you gave her your blessing for her marriage and begin a new life in a foreign land – and so was it really you, father, or was it just a dream? Forgive me, but I have always wondered.'
He gave a small nod.
'I visited her, yes, for although I had lost the power of sight I could still find my way by other means ... and such was her doubt I only did what any other man would do for the woman he loved.'
I stared down into the sunken sockets, confusion in my heart.
'What, to give her to another man..? That must have been so hard, father.'
'Give? Why, son, she was not mine to give, and I thank God that such a woman shared my life if only for a short time ... and so yes, I gave my blessing as a final act of love.' Suddenly he winced and instinctively I reached down again and laid my hands over the cruel stumps that had once been his hands.
'Is there pain? Are you in pain anywhere, father?'
'No, no pain, Jonas, just a deep ache as my soul prepares to leave this body ... but I could not depart without seeing you. Why the last time I saw you, you were but a babe ... we were both in less than fortunate circumstances, and it does my heart good to know the chance you were given has not been wasted.'
There was a long pause.
'Why didn't you come back?' I could not stop the question; it simply begged to be asked for I was overcome by an incredible sadness at all the years lost.
The drawn features creased with concern but his voice remained firm in its conviction as he made his reply.
'My one and only *precious* son ... what use would I have been to you and your mother like this, and at a time when the fight for survival was all there was? How could I have provided for you ... how could I have defended you?'
He coughed weakly before continuing.
'That day in the desert I barely escaped with my life. The devils that attacked me had left me to die like a dog in the heat ... but God was still watching over me, and soon after I was found by Aman's father ... and here I have been ever since.' I waited as he paused to get his

breath. So much talking was obviously taking its toll but he wasn't finished yet.

'They have been good to me ... so good, Jonas, and I have been blessed, despite what was taken from me, and knowing you both went on to a better life made this one easier to bear ...

More tears were threatening and I pushed them back. What could I say in the face of such selflessness! What could anyone say?

'Your mother must never know.' he added and I nodded, the knowledge would torment her forever.

I gazed down into the worn face that had not looked out on the world for twenty years; whose eyes had been ripped out and denied the blessing of being able to look upon his family again. To live out his years amongst a people who were not his own and in a land so far from home; it was heartbreaking.

'You must not feel pity for me, Jonas ... I have known only love. I have been well cared for and cherished as one of their own. It is to your life and what lies ahead that matters now, and word has it you have been doing much study.' His expression took on a wistful cast. 'Tell me, what is the Holy Land like?'

'Not as you would wish to see it, for there is much conflict there, but I venture forth little and apply myself to scriptures and debate,' I smiled in spite of myself, 'the beginnings of our bloodline continues to cause much comment. So I have come to the conclusion that Simon Magus will never be regarded as anything more than a spiritual revolutionary with questionable intent. But then they cannot disregard the evidence and so we rub along, better than I could ever have hoped.'

'Such is the way of established religion, Jonas. I may not have had the benefit of academic study as you have, but I have seen enough to know that the world is changing in a way that will need more than prayer ... but we are not alone in our quest ... we never have been. Perhaps one day you will meet others such as we are.'

'I have been told that they are out there and that our paths will one day cross. But what is most important is that I have finally met you,' I leaned down and placed a kiss on the smooth brow.

'and I would ask one last question of you, father, if I may...'

'There will never be a better time, so please, ask ...'

I drew a deep breath, aware that I was about to venture onto hallowed ground, but such was the desire within me; I simply had to know.
'Why would God devise such an end to such a noble life? You are a good man; one of his own and with such a special calling. Why was this allowed this to happen to you?'
There, it was out! My first questionable doubt that I had ever dared voice and my father then surprised me by breaking into gentle laughter as his teeth, still perfect, gleamed in the dim light of the lamp.
I waited feeling somewhat perplexed until he had finished.
'Why Jonas, my son, God only guides, he does not devise ... and it was *my* choice to walk out into the desert that day...' his voice had become breathless again, exerted by the effort, but his mirth had not been directed at me, I knew, but at the age-old question that had assailed every man who had ever walked and stumbled on the path.
'It was my choice ... my own free will, and had I turned my face away, who knows ...' his face softened but I could feel his regard upon me keenly.
'Sometimes God will take a hand when all seems lost ... that by subtle means his will, perhaps, becomes known ... and all we can do is bow to it, with no reckoning of where it will take us but ...' he smiled weakly, 'take us it will, and to unexpected places where the only light that guides us is the brightness of our faith ... and in that we must trust and know that the gifts he has given us show ... that he, too, believes in us ...'
The effort of so much speech had exhausted him and the only sound in the ensuing silence was the labouring of his breath. I gazed at him with so much love I thought it would overwhelm me for with just those few words he had removed all doubts and bending down I kissed his forehead and thanked him.
'Be at peace with what you see, and rejoice that soon I will be free of this flesh that blessed me enough to have known the love of your mother and ... the greatest blessing of all, that is you, Jonas...' he gasped for a breath now clearly struggling. 'Nearly time ... bid Samuel enter ... for I would hear the voice of my beloved brother again.'
'Yes, father.'

I rose to my feet slowly reluctant to leave, wanting to stay for every minute. But that was the yearning of a selfish need, and when I stepped out into the cold night air I cried as I had never cried before, as this noble soul who was my father made his peace with a pure and loving heart as somewhere some seven thousand miles away, the woman he still loved lived on with another man and did so with his blessing.

Chapter 18

We kept vigil for what was left of the night, Samuel and I. We each buried the intensity of our emotions to watch over and tend to the needs of my father as his life slipped slowly away.
He talked a little; of family members, his love for us, and how his passing would be all the more joyful for having us beside him.
He had no fear of what lay beyond, and seeing how serenely he accepted his fate made some way in easing the misplaced grief I was feeling.
Samuel never took his eyes from his face and listened intently, as though absorbing the very essence of his being, and as the night crept towards dawn my father made a final request.
'I would like to feel the sun on my face one last time, if I may ...' his voice was now little more than a whisper and a hint of greyness had begun to steal across the rich mahogany of his features.
'Of course,' Samuel said in a choked voice, 'and we will bear you gladly, brother.'
He looked stricken but rising up he took up the lower part of the pallet as I lifted the other, and we carefully made our way outside of the tent to be met by an extraordinary sight.
All of the Kunama tribe had assembled and were waiting silently Aman and the elders at the front. They parted as we carried my father out towards open ground and away from the camp before following at a respectful distance.
Dawn was just starting to break over the distant hills, and as we lowered the pallet carefully down to the ground, the surrounding chill began to recede immediately as the sun slowly made its ascent.
Taking up our positions once again either side of my father, Samuel and I sat quietly as the first warm rays touched our faces and sought, almost lovingly, to dry our tears.
With no conscious intent of doing so I began to hum, and as the sun rose higher still my hum became a hymn, and in the deep baritone that marked my voice, I sang an old Welsh lullaby called *Pais Dinogad* that Menna had taught me and as the words rolled richly

into the growing light I kept my eyes on my father as his face broke into a slow smile, his expression rapt.
He was still smiling when the sun finally broke free over the hilltops, and as his spirit rose and left his body I felt his passing like a gentlest touch, and looking across to Samuel I knew that he felt it too.

The Kunama tribe, who had shown such incredible care for one who had not been their own, now took up their own lament, and as the sun rose higher and higher, there we remained as we sang his spirit home; each in our own way, but united fully in the unequivocal ties of grief. The elders requested that they be allowed to accord my father their traditional rites of burial, and as he had been a part of their society for night on twenty years, neither I nor Samuel saw any reason to refuse. With great reverence the menfolk took him back to the tent, and we stood back and watched as they stripped and then washed my father's body before dressing him in a fine linen robe. Eyeliner was applied around the sunken sockets and then animal fat smoothed into the back of the head.
I felt almost detached as I observed the rites of this age-old practice, but knew in my heart that it was fitting that these people who can shown him such care be allowed to show their respect in the only way they knew how.
I glanced at Samuel whose expression was unreadable and saw him swaying slightly on his feet. The whole experience had been extraordinary and emotionally exhausting, and as neither of us had had any proper rest since our arrival, the aftermath was now beginning to show and I squeezed his arm gently.
The body now prepared and adorned with a beaded surcoat, we followed as the elders led the way to a stand of acacia trees beyond the camp.
There was a low humming as the rest of the tribe walked in our wake, and as my father was placed in the ground with great ceremony, there was peace in my heart and a strange sense of comfort.
Somehow, for all that our lives had been torn apart and then remodelled in the most unexpected of ways; I duly took comfort that God had not turned his back on my father, but had given him instead, a life that was different, but suffused nevertheless with so much love,

I could only wonder at the deep connection that had brought them all together and how keenly they felt his loss.
It was the most diverse and poignant ritual of farewell I thought I was ever likely to see, for as the Kunama sang and extolled their grief, Samuel and I held hands and prayed as three cultures came together and the spirit of my father went on his way.
No more tears were necessary. A profound gratitude filled my heart. I had been given the chance to say goodbye, and that was enough.
Tradition dictated that a feast be held in his honour, and in acknowledgment of our presence as special guests, and as the music played and voices rose in song, my uncle and I partook of the hospitality but inwardly we were exhausted and desperate for sleep. Thankfully this was recognised and after a couple of hours we were shown to a tent on the periphery of the camp where we collapsed and fell asleep almost immediately.

Aman would be taking us back over the border that night, and when dusk was falling he came to us and shook us awake.
Already the temperature was plunging as we freshened up and donned dark clothing. A quick meal with the elders to convey our gratitude was acknowledged kindly, then we were both embraced like sons before being sent on our way with their blessing.
'You will always be welcome should you ever feel a need to come visit,' Aman offered as we retrieved our bags, 'Your father will be much missed for his wisdom and gentleness of manner, but then, something tells me our paths will part this night never to meet again.'
I turned and faced this diminutive man who had risked much to cross worlds and borders, and all for the love of a man who was not even of his blood.
Holding out my hand I said softly, 'I have no doubt that our paths will cross again, but not perhaps in this one ... I thank God for you Aman and for all that you have done for my father, and for us, and should you ever need any help, then be sure to call upon Jonas Llewellyn.'
There were tears in his eyes as he clasped my hand, and then we were out and into the night as we left the fires and the tribe behind and made our way back towards the border. Aman and Kidane led from the front as before and we were to a man deep within private thought

as a pale moon rose and looked down on us.

The car was waiting where we had left it and with no sign that any patrols had been by, we hurriedly whispered our final goodbyes before pushing the car out on to the road as our companions melted away into the night.
Soon we were heading back the way we had come. The air was heavy between us and after a few miles I ventured to break the silence.
'Are you alright, uncle?'
My uncle had not said a word since bidding farewell and as I gazed at him driving behind the wheel I could sense his disquiet.
'I cannot lie, Jonas,' he replied finally, 'for I am still in a state of shock that we have seen and spoken with your father, and then the cruellest of things, to then watch him die...' he shook his head, 'It is almost beyond believable, and yet it happened; my brother, Barak, *your* father, alive all these years!'
'It is incredible, I know, and I wouldn't have believed it myself if I had not been there myself. But I give thanks to God that he didn't perish out in the desert all those years ago but knew only comfort and kindness from those who took him in. I can truly say that I feel blessed, uncle, truly I do and will carry the memories of these past couple of days safe with me forever.'
Samuel nodded.
'As will I. And so what happens now, *Assefa*?'
The shift in our relationship was not lost on me. I was not yet twenty one and yet here was my elder all but deferring to me and it marked a new stance in our relationship.
'Back to Gondar, a hotel room and some rest. We will also need to talk. There is something I wish to discuss with you and I think we both could benefit from some quality time together before I fly back.'
'You're not coming back to the village?' The surprise was evident in his voice and with it an echo of disappointment.
'It's probably best not, uncle, as much as I would like to. My priority is for us to have what little time there is and in some comfort,' I looked at him wryly, 'After the last twenty four hours or so it is the least either of us deserve!'

It was still dark when we drew into the outskirts of Gondar and were fortunate to find a decent hotel that was happy to accommodate us at such a late hour. I paid in advance for a twin room with ensuite, and after a most welcome and very hot shower we both climbed under the crisp white sheets and slipped away into the kind of deep sleep you can only dream of.

We woke at mid-morning, refreshed and feeling surreal.

'Seems to strange to think that only this time yesterday we were in another country marking the end of the life of your father,' Samuel remarked as he stretched and went to stand at the window.

There was a sound of traffic and people as the world went on around us and then turning back to me he added, 'But at least the mystery is solved now and I slept all the better for knowing he has gone home.'

I smiled pleased that he was over the residual distress, and pulling a clean robe over my head, said, 'Then let us mark this new day by finding breakfast and some good strong coffee, uncle, for I don't know about you but I'm famished!'

We spent the next few of days coming to terms to what we had just experienced, the impact of it and the speed with which we had been swept along.

'It seems almost like a dream now,' remarked Samuel time and time again until eventually we were both able to move on and talk about other things as we walked the city and drank coffee in the roadside huts.

'It has done us both good, I think, to have this time together, uncle,' I said one evening, 'but soon I must return and if I am honest, this whole experience has made me re-evaluate everything.'

Samuel looked at me askance.

'In what way? Are you having second thoughts, Jonas? I would understand if you are; it is not an easy life to lead with the devil at your heels.'

'No, no second thoughts, but what has happened has made me realise that I want to have something in my life that is ordinary ... normal ... an aspect that isn't coloured by mysticism and endless study.'

'You are talking about your young woman.'

'I am, and there can be no one else for me but Menna. She understands me and what it's all about, and I would be hard pressed to find another like her and notwithstanding, know I would trust her with my life.'

'Is this what you wanted to talk to me about, *Assefa?*' Samuel kept his voice neutral as he topped up our cups from the pot and added sugar.

'Yes. Seeing my father lying in that tent so far from home, away from the very heart of his family made me realise just how nothing is guaranteed - not even when you have the eye of the Lord upon you. I intend to name a date as soon as I return, but there will be opposition from within the family, I know, and as one who has always been considerate of me and my interests; I would ask you now would you do the same if you were in my shoes?'

My uncle stirred his cup thoughtfully and watching him in profile for the first time I could see the resemblance to my father and as ever I felt a slight pang.

'It is a shame that you could not have asked this question of your father, for it was he who married for love and would've been able to give you a better answer. Me? I never married as you know, Jonas, and have never felt the desire to do so, therefore I will confess I am the wrong person to ask, but that is not to say I do not have an answer at all.'

'Which is ..?'

'Go with your heart, but know there may be consequences. Look at your mother, seemingly widowed and with you still on the hip, and who knows where either of you would be if it had not been for your stepfather. Just know that there are risks for those who walk the path, and that you must never, *ever,* let your guard down no matter the circumstances.'

I nodded and my mind flitted back to the attack in Rome. I knew what he was saying was true. But I was still a young man and with a young man's desires; they just didn't rule me, but that wasn't to say I wasn't pulled by their draw.

'I hear you, uncle, and believe me I would protect her with my life. Often, I admit, when I'm surrounded by books and my mind is in the past, just to be able to relax at the end of the day with a meal and good company from someone that wants nothing from me other than me; to be able to laugh and talk of things not associated with scripture

or religious debate. To be able to sing, banter and...'
'Make love,' Samuel interjected and I felt myself blush.
He reached across the table and placed a hand on my forearm his expression grave.
'*Assefa*, I understand what it is you are saying, really I do, and I'm not saying that you cannot have any of these things. But your life will never be anything less than extraordinary, and never quite your own. Your calling will drive and compel you, whether you want it or not, and such will be your attraction, there will always be those that will seek to do you harm." He drew back. "The bigger the purpose, the greater the shine ... I don't think I need to spell it out.'
'I will protect her,' I said doggedly, 'even if it means with my life.'
'Then be sure to keep up with all of your skills, including the fighting ones, because if you are really set on marrying your Menna, you will need everything at your disposal and more than the blessing of God. The world is not what it was; everything is changing, shifting, moving into darker times and where there is darkness, bad things bide their time and become ever bolder, people more corruptible, and the Devil, as we know, is not choosey about what company he keeps.'
He placed his cup back into its saucer and gave me a firm look.
'Have your Menna if that is your wish and know that I will support you and the reasoning for your choice. Just keep your guard high and trust no one. No one, Jonas! All I ask is that you look to and remember the fate of your father.'
I held his gaze and for a moment and it was as though I saw my father looking out and I acknowledged his warning with a dip of my head.
'I hear you, dear uncle, and your counsel to me is sound in its wisdom as ever and I give you my word, as God is my witness, that I will never falter in my regard for her safety; and that should I fail may the good Lord strike me down and seal my lips forever.'
Samuel lifted an eyebrow and then turned his face away.
'Then just let us hope that it doesn't come to that, eh, *Assefa, b*ecause you have a fine singing voice and that would be a shame.'

Chapter 19

I returned to Wales and a rapturous welcome from my family who had not been expecting me. Menna was less welcoming and still slightly chilly when I spoke to her on the phone but a thaw set in swiftly as soon as I relayed my intentions.
Her gasp of pleasure was like music to my ears.
'What! You want to set a date?'
'I don't see the point in delaying. We're been engaged long enough. Do you want me to be with you when you tell your parents? I can be there by tomorrow evening, I just need some time to break the news my end.'
'No, no, I'll be fine! Oh Jonas, I can't believe this is happening, I'm finally going to be Mrs Llewellyn! She laughed delightedly. 'But where shall we be married? Here in Bala, I suppose!'
'I was thinking more Bangor Cathedral, if that sits well with you...'
'Sits well with me? *Sits well with me?* Are you having a laugh, Jonas!'
Her joy was infectious and I was smiling broadly as I came off the phone with lightness in my heart I hadn't felt in a long time.
I turned round to find my mother stood in the doorway watching me.
'Bangor Cathedral, eh ... and so when were you going to tell us? And more importantly, what has brought this on, Jonas?'
My smile faltered. My mother had that look in her eye and I knew that she knew *something.*
'Why has anything had to have happened for me to want to marry the girl I love! We have known each other long enough and she deserves a special day. I was thinking a quiet ceremony in the cathedral courtesy of the canon, of course, but it is an apt choice as Menna and I met in Bangor after all.'
I went across and put my arm her.
'Oh mother, be happy for me, please! You have that look when someone sings out of tune and I don't think I can bear it!' My tone was bright and cajoling and she looked up at me searchingly.
'I would not deny you happiness, Jonas, me least of anyone. But your

haste worries me. What has happened, why did you have to go with such secrecy, and now why the rush to get married?'

I looked down into the smooth lines of her face. She had barely aged in all the years since embarking on our new life and was as striking as ever, even the grey strands that had began to touch her temples only emphasized her beauty.

The sightless gaze of my father passed through my mind and I could only imagine how many times the memory of my mother must've remained with him all those years like a tantalising dream and the thought strengthened my resolve.

'You more than anyone have my confidence, and truly, if I could tell you I would. But you also know that there are some things that remain between me and God and that these I cannot divulge.'

I dropped a kiss on to her brow, 'I am a man now, Mother, and have learned of such things as to change my view of the world forever. But I also have need of companionship beyond the long-lost voices I find in study, and Menna is good for me. She makes me happy and she keeps me grounded. Let me have your blessing, please, and with it the hope we will enjoy as happy a life as you do.'

She shook her head slowly a small smile on her lips, 'Ah my *Assefa*, all grown up and dictating to his mother, but you are resolved on this, I see. So what other cause is there open to me? Of course I will give you my blessing but I will also warn you to take care.'

With a sudden fierceness she drew me to her.

'You forget the particulars of my beginning. My father and those who came before him practiced the art of medicine and so I have enough understanding to know a few things myself ... something *has* happened but I will hold my peace. Just don't let it drive you, Jonas, stay true to the path and what you are here for and know that sometimes, love is not for everyone.'

Before I could make comment Rhys stepped into the room.

'Ah so this is where you're hiding! Having a mother and son moment are you?'

The years had been less kind to my stepfather. He was still a fine-looking man, but he had thickened around the middle and his salt and pepper fair was all but completely white.

I pulled back and looked down at my mother. The oddness of her

remark had been duly noted but I filed it away to consider later.
'I have been sharing the good news. Perhaps you could like to announce it?'
Her dark eyes flashed momentarily and then turning smoothly to face my stepfather she said, 'You'd best see about getting me a new hat, Rhys, for it looks as though Jonas is finally going to make an honest woman of Menna!'
Aware that the news was as disquieting as it was unexpected he made the best of it nevertheless and gave me his customary slap on the back before congratulating me.
'Well you certainly know how to keep us on our toes, Jonas!' he said brightly, 'I'd best dig my old suit out for cleaning and see about a new pair of shoes if your mother's going to have a new hat!'

The formal arrangements followed on swiftly, I made sure of that. Menna was equally keen and we set a date for the fourth of December.
'A winter wedding, then?' Menna's mother had remarked over a rather strained afternoon tea, 'and where do you propose to set up home then, Jonas, in the Vatican?'
'Mam!'
'It's alright, Menna. The diocese has kindly offered us one of their parish cottages just outside the town for a reasonable rent,' I had replied placatingly, 'although His Holiness did offer, but I had to turn him down.'
My future mother-in-law's lips quirked and I knew she'd come round as would Menna's father who was wrapped around his daughter's finger. Steffan, predictably, was as pleased as punch. We had always got on well and he liked the idea of having such an exotic new addition to the family.
'You're not like anyone else, Jonas, but you've always been a good friend to me, and I know you'll take care of my sister,' he had said upon hearing the news. 'Just don't let her boss you round too much!'
We'd laughed for we both knew Menna to be the more dominant of the two and it was only natural we that we choose Steffan as our best man. We had decided on a much muted affair with just a few guests. Permission had been granted to get married in the beautiful old

cathedral, the banns had been issued and everything was set; all we had to do was wait for the big day.

Winter had come early just a few days before with plummeting temperatures and the threat of heavy snow.

'Are you sure you want to go up to Snowdonia for your honeymoon?' My mother questioned one evening over the phone, 'I just hope the weather doesn't set in before we get a chance to get up there. I said to Rhys, perhaps we'd best come up a day or so sooner Just to be sure.'

'Whatever you think is best,' I said, 'and as to your concerns about our honeymoon, the cottage is all booked now and we're both looking forward to it. Menna has arranged for provisions and the farmer who owns it lives just down the road. We'll be fine.'

'Well, it'll certainly be romantic,' my mother teased. 'Snowed in on your honeymoon, we might not see you again until the spring!'

She too, had finally come round to the idea of my marriage and had thrown herself into the preparations.

'Your father and I had quite a different start to married life,' she went on and I heard the wistful tone in her voice, 'we honeymooned up in the Simien Mountains, it was just before high summer and we made camp in a wonderful little cave. Indeed it was where you were conceived, Jonas, for we were very much in love and your father was such a *passionate* man!'

I had an image of my father dying slowly beneath brightly-woven blankets in an unknown land, tended to and cherished by an adopted tribe. Weak, wasting, and waiting patiently for death. I pushed the image away from my mind; may my mother always remember him as he was.

The ceremony was short and simple and performed in the early afternoon. With just close family members we retired to a local hotel to celebrate, and I had never seen Menna look so happy or so stunning. Dressed in a plain woollen dress of winter white, her titian hair was pinned up beneath the sequinned hood and she looked like some Celtic princess of legend who had deigned to walk among us and my heart nearly burst with pride.

Her hazel eyes were shining as we drank a toast, but I only took the one sip as we would soon be heading up into the solace of the

Snowdonia in our collective wedding present.

'You must have a car,' Menna's father had decreed as he handed over the keys, 'It's well-nigh impossible to function up here without one, as you know! So we've all clubbed together and got you this four by four; it's not brand new, but it's a good runner with low mileage and we've also sorted the insurance.'

As Menna hugged him I beamed with delight as our bags were loaded and a couple of bottles of champagne stashed in for good measure.

'For later,' said Steffan with a wink and I don't think I'd ever been so happy.

My old tutor Einion stepped forward. Having sent him an invitation I wasn't sure he would attend, but he was genuinely pleased to have been asked and proffered his hand almost shyly.

'*Cyfarchion,* Jonas,' he murmured, 'May God's blessing be upon you - always.'

It was a double entendre and an indication that he was at peace with what I was about and I dispensed with my usual reserve and gave him a hug.

'Why put him down, Jonas, before you squeeze him to death!' My mother cried and then in a quiet aside added, 'You look so handsome, so like your father. He would've been *so* proud of you. As I am, as we all are. Enjoy your time with Menna, and, be gentle...'

Further embarrassment was spared as my siblings now demanded a hug and it was a merry gathering that saw us off as the first flakes of snow began to fall amidst the growing dusk.

'Take care on the roads and call us when you get back!' shouted Menna's mother as we pulled away, and hearing the inevitable rattle of wedding regalia behind us we waited until we were out of sight before stopping to remove them.

'Oh Jonas,' laughed Menna as we untied the medley of cans the snow blowing around us, 'I can't believe we're finally married, and just look at all of this snow! Did you arrange for this on order or is it just a fluke?'

Throwing the now silent receptacles into the boot I turned and drew her up into my arms.

'Why, are you complaining, Mrs Llewellyn?'

She laughed some more before rubbing my nose with her cold one.

'Absolutely not, Mr Llewellyn, I wouldn't dare! But the way it's coming down we'd better not hang around, eh? Not if we want to sleep in a warm bed tonight!'

We kissed deeply and then I released her as I felt the heat rise deep in my loins. It just all seemed so utterly perfect. My beautiful new bride, an isolated retreat in which to discover each other; and in one of the most natural and magical places in the world. *Eryri* - 'Land of the Eagles.'

We had chosen to stay in a remote cottage not far from the village of Beddgelert that nestled in the foothills of Wales's most famous mountain range.

Like Menna I had a great love for the area and we wanted to spend our precious time together in an idyllic setting far from crowds and noisy places. We chatted gaily as we passed through Caernarfon before turning right up towards Rhyd Ddu and our destination.

'So what did your mother whisper to you as we were leaving?' enquired Menna mischievously.

'Oh just mother-son stuff, you know how it is.'

She tutted and gave my arm a playful punch.

'No, go on, what was it? I want to know – there can be no secrets between us now that we're married.'

'Yes, and we haven't been married five minutes before you're making wifely demands!' I countered with mock exasperation.

'Aye, as you will be making 'husbandly' demands shortly, no doubt.' she returned pertly slanting her eyes.

I laughed and felt a stirring that would soon be assuaged as both the woman I loved and I sealed our union, and reaching out I took her hand and kissed it.

'Thank you, Menna. For waiting for me and for, well, just being you.'

'No, Jonas,' she said suddenly solemn, 'thank you for choosing me, and trusting me enough to share the wonder that is you, *cariad*. I feel truly blessed and it is my belief that we will have a very interesting life together.'

I released her hand and returned it to the wheel as the road began to curve. The snow was still falling but more gently and my heart was singing.

'Then that makes two of us. I love you, Menna. I never thought it

would be possible to love anyone as much as I love you.'
'Then tell me what your mother said!' she returned quick as a flash and we both laughed.
'Nothing for you to worry about, *cariad*, just along the lines of a reminder to be remain a gentleman, little more than that.'
'But not *too* much of a *gentleman*, I hope, Jonas ...' she murmured and I felt myself blush furiously. But that was one of the things I loved about her. Her boldness, her propensity to dispense with propriety and just be herself.
'You are shameless, woman! Good job we're not staying in the Vatican because the walls have ears there, you know!'
'They do? Well that's alright because they can keep them, I'd much rather have our honeymoon in Wales, oh, and look! There's the sign, we're here!'
She turned to me her eyes bright and I was caught up in her excitement.
We turned off the main road and climbed up and away from the pretty village that was twinkling with lights like some scene from a winter fairytale. We came to a farm on our left and I stopped to retrieve the key that had been left under an old milk churn.
'About three miles and then off to the right, the farmer said.'
The snow was now falling in earnest but the car climbed steadily as I kept it in low gear and soon we saw a light shining in the distance.
'That must be it!' cried Menna brandishing the key, 'the old shepherd hut!'
'The much extended and luxurious version, I'll have you know!' I corrected her playfully, 'As if I'd take my wife to a basic hut with just wooden floors and an old sheepskin to lie on!'
Once again she took my breath away by slanting those eyes and in low passionate tones saying, 'And still I would, even without the sheepskin.'
I turned up the rutted track that was fast filling with snow as it came down ever thicker, and as we pulled up at the side of the squat stone building the source of the light was a hurricane lamp that glowed softly in the window.
'We're here and none too soon by the looks of it! Stay here for a moment, if you please, Mrs Llewellyn, while I unlock the door and I

will be back for you directly.'
Menna giggled as I bent against the wind and swiftly made my way to the door and placed the key in the lock. I gave it a turn and then with a flourish made my way back to the car and for my wife.
As she got out still giggling I swept her up in my arms as the snow whipped around us and I pretended to stagger as the wind pushed and buffeted against us.
'Jonas I have to say, I never thought I would be carried over the threshold in a force ten blizzard!' cried Menna in delight.
'Well you did say you believed our marriage would be interesting, so where better to start!' I returned laughingly, and as I pushed at the door and the wind blew us in, we heard it and in an instant the laughter dried on our lips as we froze into silence and stared at each other.
No, surely, it couldn't be ...

Chapter 20

The sound came again, faint but unmistakable, and I swung round swiftly shutting the door behind us with a loud thud.
'Did you hear that? *Did you hear that!*'
Menna's voice was incredulous, her eyes wide and she kept them on me as I lowered her slowly down to the floor.
We stared at each other before I gathered myself and reached out with my mind. There was nothing but snow and wind as it moaned its ceaseless song and finally with a small laugh I found my voice.
'There are no wolves in Wales, are there?'
I felt stupid for asking the question, of course there were not. Yet I know what I had heard.
What we both heard!
'No, no, of course not! If my memory serves me correct, the last wolf was killed in Cregina near Builth Wells and that was *centuries* ago! It's probably a farm dog out in the snow - either that or the wind.' But her tone was unconvinced.
The nearest farm was the one we'd passed for the key and that was three miles away, but I said nothing. Already Menna was visibly recovering herself as she looked around the small cosy interior before giving a squeal of pleasure.
'Oh look, Jonas, a wood burner! Shaking the snow from her hooded cape she threw it to one side before bending down to the hearth and the stack of logs, 'How nice that the farmer has got it going for us, but it'll need more wood and fast. I'll stoke up the fire whilst you get the bags. Oh, and don't forget the champagne!'
I smiled in spite of myself. She was, as usual, infectious in her enthusiasm but something told me to be on my guard. As I retrieved our luggage from the car I stood listening for some moments as the snow billowed about driven by a furious wind until the intense cold drove me back inside.
It was now nearly pitch-dark and difficult to see anything of the valley below. I knew from the pictures that we were quite high up, but the driving snow and the dying light made anything visual

impossible.

Menna had got the fire blazing and suddenly appeared from behind a beaded curtain smiling broadly.

'There is the sweetest little kitchen and a good-sized bathroom at the back,' she announced happily all thoughts of howling wolves seemingly forgotten. 'It's perfect, Jonas! How cosy are we going to be all *cwtched* up in here?'

I followed her eyes up to the gallery bedroom and could see the snow swirling beyond the two skylights.

'It's going to be *so* romantic, Jonas! Here, let me take that fizz and I'll find us some glasses. Just dump the bags, *cariad,* we can see to those later.'

I did as I was told and then sat myself down on to the generous couch that spanned the hearth. The heat from the wood stove hit me immediately and I eased back relishing the warmth as Menna appeared carrying two bubbling champagne flutes.

With great ceremony we cracked open one of the bottles and after toasting each other accordingly, settled back against each other as the flames of the fire danced before us.

After the drive and such a frenetic, although highly enjoyable day, we were content to just sit quietly for a while and savour the moment as the wind howled and raged outside.

'Wow, that really is turning into some storm.' remarked Menna snuggling against me, 'but I don't care! We have a fridge full of food, lots more of this lovely fizz, and ...' she leaned up and pecked me on the lips, 'each other!'

There must've been traces of disquiet in my eyes because now she leaned back so as to regard me properly.

'I know that look, what is it, Jonas? You're not still worrying about that strange howling, are you? As I said it's probably just the wind, or else some dog that doesn't like the weather!'

'Then if it is a dog that's been left outside shouldn't we be concerned?'

'No, *cariad,* because if it a dog from down the road, the wind will be making it sound nearer than what it is. Trust me, no farmer would leave his dog out in these conditions.'

She had already decided on an explanation and that was that.

'Here,' she said topping up our glasses, 'I'll tell you a story about a dog that's very famous in these parts. It's always been my favourite and I also know you'll also like it because the prince in it has the same name to you!'
I settled back bemused by her philosophy. I knew the tale of course, but why spoil the moment.
Tucking her feet in beneath her she began.
'Long ago when wolves roamed the land and Wales was ruled by its own prince, one called Prince Llywelyn held court in these parts. Like all royalty he loved the hunt, and of all his many hunting hounds his favourite was called Gelert. One day the Llywelyn decided to go outhunting, and as his wife had recently given birth he left the faithful Gelert behind to guard his new-born son.
Some hours later on the Prince's return, he hastened to the nursery only to be presented with a most terrible sight! The cradle had been knocked over and there was blood all over Gelert's face. Assailed by the notion that his dog had killed his son, Llywelyn drew his sword and slew Gelert on the spot! And then as poor dog lay dying the Prince heard the cry of a baby. He lifted the cradle only to find his son safe and well, and beyond it half-hidden by the covers, the dead body of a wolf!
He wept as he realised what had really happened. His fearless and most beloved Gelert had not killed the baby after all, but had fought the ravening wolf to the death and saved the life of his son!
He was heartbroken, but he had struck a mortal blow and nothing could be done to save poor Gelert.
In honour of this most faithful hound the Prince buried him just outside the walls of the *Llys* and decreed ever after that this place be known as *Beddgelert.* And so it is to this day; translated it means 'the grave of Gelert' and legend has it there he rests still.'
Menna looked towards the fire and I could see tears glistening in the corner of her eyes and I understood. The story of Gelert had that effect no matter how many times you heard it.
'A sad tale for a wedding night, *cariad,* but beautifully told, it has to be said,'
I reached out and stroked her cheek and then as though struck by a sudden though she turned back to me, her eyes bright.

'You would know, wouldn't you? *Of course you'd know!*'
I stared at her perplexed.
'Know what, Menna?'
Her lovely face had become animated and I marvelled as ever at the landscape of ever-changing emotions of this woman. Tears one minute, excitement the next.
'Gelert - the grave! If he is really in there? Tell me, Jonas, because I think you'd know. Is the legend true, or is it just a stone and a tragic tale to fool the tourists?'
I dropped my gaze.
I had visited Beddgelert once many years ago with Einion before such excursions became the norm with Menna and her brother, and had stood before the alleged final resting place of this fabled hound, and had felt ... *something...*
I looked up and Menna's eyes were on me like a gimlet. I gave a small nod and she let out a hoot of delight, 'I knew it! *I knew it!'*
I laughed at her childlike pleasure before saying, 'Come here, you crazy woman, I want to kiss my wife!'
As she drew into me and our lips met, the moment was arrested as there came from the door a very loud knock and we sprang back from each other in shock.
The wind moaned in the silence that followed and then the knock came again.
'Jonas, there's someone at the door!' Menna breathed incredulously, her eyes huge. 'Who could it be and out in this weather?'
I passed her my glass and without further ado stood up and retrieved my wooden cross where I had left it atop of the luggage. With a quick flick I extended it into the staff and it seemed to thrum into life as though it had been waiting.
Quietly I went across to the door and listened.
The wind moaned as though desperate to seek entrance but no other sound reached my ears. I was aware, however, that something or *someone* was there, and that it, too, was listening just as intently.
I looked at Menna and put a finger to my lips and then waited as the sound of the wind wailed and cajoled me to open the door.
I had no intention of doing so.
If our unexpected visitor was genuine, like a walker who might have

been caught out by the weather, for instance, they would be aware that their sudden appearance might cause alarm and would have seen fit to call out as they knocked. We were half-way up a mountain with a blizzard raging outside, and as I kept my ear to the door one of Shakespeare's most famous lines came into my mind; *There are more things in heaven and earth, Horatio, than are dreamt of in your philosophy ...*

And hell, I thought grimly.

There were two bolts on the door and I now drew them across. The key, thankfully, I'd had the mind to bring in when I'd returned with the bags, and as I turned it quietly in the well-oiled lock the handle began to slowly turn and I felt my heartbeat quicken.

Whatever it was and I had no doubt it wasn't anything human, it certainly did not lack for boldness.

Swiftly I went around and drew all of the curtains as Menna watched me open-mouthed with rising dismay.

'Jonas, what's ...' she began and this time I placed my finger on her lips as I resumed my seat next to her.

'It would appear we have company.' I said in a low voice, 'but whatever you do, you mustn't panic. Neither must you, under any circumstances, open that door...' I gave her a meaningful look, 'No matter what, or who you might hear from outside it.'

She nodded, all wedded bliss and laughter gone, and then fumbling in her bag she drew out her phone.

'No signal,' Her whisper was sibilant in its urgency and I took her hands in mine.

'Menna, you must keep a cool head. Whatever it is it can't get in, and the storm has probably knocked out the signal. We'll just have to sit tight, but know that we're quite safe.'

'Quite? Hardly reassuring, Jonas!' she countered with a touch of her old spirit.

'Sorry, wrong use of vocabulary. *Cariad,* you *are* safe, *very* safe. I won't let anything hurt you, I promise.'

That seemed to appease her and taking a deep breath nodded her head towards the door. The handle had stopped turning but I knew with a deep certainty that whatever it was remained outside. Waiting.

'So who...what is it, do you know?'

'Elementals, I'm thinking. They're natural energies but highly inquisitive and mischievous too. The storm has probably brought them out.'

'And you ...' It was a statement of fact and we both knew it.

'Yes, and me, quite possibly.' I agreed.

'But they are not looking to hurt us?'

I shook my head but on this I couldn't be sure. My inherent sense of *knowing* had identified them for what they were; but how much they had evolved and to what purpose I could not tell. Not without direct contact and it was too risky to even consider that option.

'And so we wait!'

I watched as Menna drew away and retrieved the bottle and as she went to refill my glass I put my hand across it firmly.

'No, cariad, no more for me tonight.'

She shrugged and filled up her own instead.

'Ah well, all the more for me then as the local ghosties and ghoulies ruin my night, because I can see from your face that there'll be no sleep for either of us, never mind the *other!*'

'Sorry Menna,' I said tenderly and she waved a hand.

'It's no matter, we've waited this long I'm sure we can wait a bit longer. Besides we have the rest of our married life together, and so, if you don't mind, husband, I intend to imbibe a few spirits of my own as it's still my wedding night and tradition, I believe demands the wife gets pissed!'

She was making light of the situation, I knew, and seeing how quickly she drained her glass alarmed me but for the second time that night I held my peace. If that was the only way in which she could deal with what was happening, then so be it. But I would keep a covert eye.

A scratching sound came from outside the door and another near to the window, but it was the sound that followed which chilled me to the bone as a loud howl rent the air before being carried away by the wind.

This time there could be no mistaking it.

We stared at each other for some moments and then Menna raised an eyebrow saying, 'That was no elemental, Jonas. In fact that wasn't even a *dog!*'

'I know.'

'So then what is happening?' There was just the slightest edge of panic to her voice and I put a finger to my lips as I began to rise from the settee.

'No! *Don't!*' Menna grabbed at my leg with a fierceness that surprised me.

'Menna...'

'No!'

She poured more champagne with a hand that was shaking and I could only watch helplessly as she drank the entire contents before emitting a small hiccup.

'Jonas, please, whatever is out there, don't let it ... don't encourage it by acknowledging it ... *please!'*

I knew what she meant, of course, Menna was not without a good sensitivity but I had to *know*.

'Just a quick look out of the window, *cariad,* I promise and then ...'

'Jonas, *don't!'* Menna broke in vehemently, 'because if you acknowledge it, you encourage it ... isn't that what you've always told me?'

Dismayed I gazed at her as she swayed slightly and her eyes gave a small roll. She was unaccustomed to drinking anything more modest than the odd glass of wine and she had just drank the best part of a bottle.

'It's alright, Menna,' I said soothingly, 'if it bothers you that much I'll stay here with you.'

'It does,' she slurred, 'maybe if we ignore them they'll go away.'

There was little likelihood of that as another howl called mournfully out into the night and leaning forward I threw more logs on the fire as my mind worked furiously.

I had read about Elementals, of course, their place in mythology, their ancient lineage and connection to the land, but I would never have expected to encounter them like this! And what was their purpose? What did they want? Were they being driven by something darker? Or had my presence and the storm disturbed them from sleep and they were now bent on creating havoc.

The fact we were hearing the sounds of wolves howling did not mean that such creatures were actually out there. The Elementals were not

unlike the *Jinn* in that they could take the form and mimic all manner of beings. But without actually be able look outside and investigate further I was not willing to underestimate what might be out there. More scratching came from the door and Menna giggled.
'Maybe it's the wolf that fought Gelert ... come back to wreak revenge.'
Her behaviour was starting to concern me, but then the circumstances were far from ordinary. A bride's night was supposed to be one of the most special of their life, and yet faced with such strange phenomena most women would probably have become hysterical, or else gone screaming into the night.
'What about something to eat, Menna? It might help.' I raised a smile trying to introduce some much-needed normality
She giggled again.
'No, you're alright, Jonas, this champagne is doing the job perfectly. Who'd have thought we'd be spending our wedding night trapped in a shepherd's hut halfway up a mountain being ...' she paused and hiccupped, 'serenaded by a pack of wolves ... only you, *cariad* ...'
I went and got a blanket and wrapped it around her shoulders.
'Don't lose it, Menna,' I murmured drawing her close, 'whatever you do, don't lose it, *cariad*.'
Her hair smelled of fresh herbs and I concentrated on emanating a calm energy as she nestled against me.
'I know... I won't, I promise,' she took a deep warbling breath as the wind moaned mournfully as though in sympathy. 'I guess I just wasn't expecting it to start so soon.'
'I know, Menna, but we are safe as long as we stay inside.'
At those words my mind touched back on similar reassurances given that first night up in the Simien Mountains and Samuel's unconcern of what waited outside. But then the cave was under celestial protection. Did this divine intervention extend to wherever I might be?
I remembered the night in Rome and somehow I thought not. The cave had been a holy place; this was merely a stone-built shelter for hardy souls who had once tended a flock of an entirely different kind. But they still couldn't come in – not unless they were invited.
Another howl sallied forth into the night and was answered by

another some distance away. *Iesu Grist, how many were there out there!*

The wrinkle in Menna's brow echoed the same question and in a bid to distract her I pointed to the bookshelf. A small cd player sat atop a stack of various paperbacks and board-games and the sight of it was like a *manna* from heaven.

'You see that CD player over there? I'm going to find something decent and we'll have a slow dance. How would you like that, Mrs Llewellyn?'

She looked up at me her mouth comically half-open.

'*What?* We are going to have a dance whilst the hounds from hell keep us prisoner? Ssseriously, Jonas..?' I smiled as she slurred and dropped a quick kiss onto her furrowed brow.

'Yes, why not? Whatever it is that's outside may've distracted me from taking my congenial rights; but I'll be damned if they'll deny me the first dance with my wife!'

As I rifled through the complimentary selection I came across the greatest hits of Sade and turned up the volume as the smooth tones began cooing, 'Your love is King.'

I held out my hand to Menna and she stood up and tottered into my arms.

There came a sound of a scuffle from the door and a sudden growl and inwardly I sighed.

It was going to be a long night.

Chapter 21

After a few gentle turns on our makeshift dance floor, Menna began to yawn as the wine and the day's events began to make themselves felt, and she made no complaint as I led her back to the couch.
'That's it, *cariad,* stretch out and try to relax, I'll be watching over you all night.'
'Promise..?' she breathed.
Her eyes already closing as I tucked the blanket around her before stroking her lovely face.
She was slightly flushed and her hair in all its amber glory had become loose, and the tale of Sleeping Beauty came to mind as I kissed the gently parted lips.
'And hope to die ... now sleep my most beautiful *cariad,* and I promise you everything will be alright in the morning.'
As soon as her breathing relaxed into a deep slumber, I rose and made my way quietly to the window that didn't have the lamp. Of the two that flanked the main entrance, I would have a better chance to see what lie beyond and pulling the edge of the curtain back I carefully peered out.
It took a while for my eyes to become adjusted to the contrast as the snow, whipped about wildly by the wind, made any kind of clarity difficult. But after a while I detected dark shadows that were moving about, but when I'd turn to bring them to the centre of my eye, they melted away.
I let the curtain fall back and looked back to the hearth as the fire glowed invitingly as though all was as it should be and was well with the world.
But I knew it was not, and that as soon as it was light and safe to do so, we would be making a swift exit. There were lots of hotels and guest-houses in the area and I was confident we'd find somewhere suitable for the rest of our honeymoon.
Our honeymoon...
I returned to the couch and gazed down at Menna as she quietly found solace in sleep, and how long we'd both waited for this night. But it

was not to be, and as she herself had said; we'll have the rest of our lives together.
As she drowsed and dreamt, I sat and waited as the hours ticked slowly past, and when the first signs of dawn began to seep through the skylights the noises from without faded away.
I went out to the little kitchen at the back and put the kettle on.
Menna was less than keen to be roused so early, and it was a snowy dawn that greeted us as I drew back the curtains my eyes searching for signs of our nocturnal visitors.
A lone robin sat on the branch of a tree that marked the beginning of the woods as they sloped down towards the valley. We eyed each other for some moments before it flew off and I opened the door for a closer look and was filled with dismay.
Not because there was not so much of a print or a ripple in the swathes of pristine snow, but because the snow itself had been busy in the night and we were effectively snowed in. I looked across to where I had parked the car and it was a vague white shape that would take ages to dig out with no guarantee of it even starting.
'Oh shut that door, Jonas! It's freezing in here!'
I did as I was told and stoked up the fire. The log supply had run low, not that it mattered. We would not be staying any longer than was necessary.
I looked at Menna. She had disappeared back beneath the blankets, her mug of tea untouched.
'Menna, you have you get up. We can't stay here.'
Her eyes fluttered and one hand rose to her head.
'I feel dreadful ... why did you let me drink so much champagne...'
I sat down next to her.
'Do you remember anything about last night, Menna?'
Her eyes opened and they rested on me blearily.
'Oh Jonas, how could I forget? Gelert's wolf!
'It wasn't Gelert's wolf, Menna, but there were things that had no business being here and we have to get out because it goes without saying they'll be back again tonight.'
She gave a half-hearted laugh.
'No business being here! Oh Jonas, these mountains have had *things* here for more years than anyone would care to remember, if all the

myths are to be believed ... you know the *Mabinogion,* you know the tales.'

'Fairytales, Menna, with perhaps one or two loosely based on fact, now come on, *cariad*, I need you to rouse yourself because although the snow has stopped for now, the sky still looks heavy and we need to go... *now.*'

She wrinkled her brow.

'Where?'

She was in a worse state than I realised and if ever I needed her to be her bright sparky self it was now.

'To the farm, we need help to get the car out but as soon as that's done we can be on our way.'

'You mean walk? *Walk down to the farm!'* Her tone was aghast at the very notion.

'No, you're quite right I'll sprout some wings and fly us down instead!'

I was beginning to lose patience. I was tired but still keyed up, and as Menna gazed up at me reproachfully I was immediately filled with shame.

'I'm sorry, *cariad,* I didn't mean it. I'm more tired than I thought and have allowed worry to get the better of me. Yes, we are going to have to walk, I'm afraid. There is no other way.'

She closed her eyes and turned on her side drawing the blankets up beneath her chin.

'Then you'll have to carry me, Jonas, because I'm not going anywhere the way I'm feeling right now, not on foot, not on anything...' she snuggled down further, 'just stoke up the fire and come back for me. Believe me, I'm not going anywhere.'

I stared down at her, her face half-hidden by her hair and for the first time in my life I was assailed by a queasiness of doubt.

Would she be okay? Was it safe to leave her? I'd promised to protect her with my life, but how could I if I left her on her own?

I chewed on my lip uncertainly. Surely now with dawn well and truly underway whatever had visited during the night was long gone, and if she locked the door behind me ...

'Menna.'

She stirred and mumbled something.

'*Menna!*'
One eye opened and I reached down and smoothed her hair.
'*Cariad,* I really don't want to leave you here and perhaps if you tried a little toast with some tea you'll feel a bit better,' I made my voice light but inwardly I was in conflict. At least try, and besides, what happened to *love, honour and obey?* And to think you only took your vows yesterday!'
I was deliberately baiting her, but I didn't know what else to do. In reply she lifted her head long enough to give me sour look.
'Don't you start all that nonsense with me, Jonas Llewellyn, because dragging your newly-wed bride miles through the snow is hardly on a par with *I promise to love and cherish,* is it? So just you leave me here and I'll be fine ... I'd probably hold you up anyway!'
With a loud harrumph she dropped her head back down to the cushion and I knew the decision had been made.
'Okay then lock the door behind me and draw the bolts. Can you rally yourself enough to do that? Menna, come on, wake up properly and work with me here!'
I could feel a rising tide of irritation threatening to overcome me and hated myself for it. But even after all that had happened the night before she seemed oblivious to the danger. All the more reason not to leave her but I couldn't insist she come with me. Not unless I threw her over my shoulder and carried her like some Neanderthal, and that wasn't my style.
I glanced towards the windows where just a few gentle flakes meandered through the still air. It was now fully light and there was no time for delay.
I went to our bags and pulled out warm thick clothing and my sturdy new walking boots. Thankfully we'd come prepared so I was able to wrap up appropriately for the long cold trudge ahead, and as much as I didn't like to admit it, Menna was right; I would be far quicker on my own and not for the first time in my life I thanked God for my height and long legs.
As I changed I silently prayed for his vigilance to keep watch over my Menna. I also reached out to my father and asked his soul come close and guard the woman of my heart.
I felt a deep uneasiness at leaving her, but I'd envisaged a ring of

protection that would remain in place for as long as I was away. As long as Menna stayed warm and inside she would be safe.

I stoked up the fire with more logs and inwardly thanked the farmer for his foresight in keeping a good stock indoors and then gently shook Menna from her nest.

'Cariad, wake up. I am going now, but you must lock the door behind me. Come on, wake up, Menna!'

With a groan she pulled herself to and with her hair tumbling and her eyes slanted with sleep, she looked both vulnerable and beautiful and I swooped down and gave her a kiss.

She wound her arms around my neck and murmured, 'Come on, Jonas, just lay down with me for a bit ... it's still early and I could do with a nice, warm *cwtch.*'

I drew back. I would've loved nothing more, and she looked so inviting, so sensual with her red hair against the creamy white of her dress.

'Ahhh, you temptress, Mrs Llewellyn! What man wouldn't want to cwtch with you and do more! But this one will have to wait if we are to be out of this place before any more of this snow makes it impossible.'

I stood up and held out my hand and Menna pushed back the blankets grumbling under her breath.

'Do not open the door to anyone other than myself, and I promise I will be as quick as I can. Promise me, Menna!'

She shuffled behind me as I drew her towards the door and for the first time I noticed how small her hand was clasped in mine.

'I will promise you anything, Jonas, just let a poor girl sleep!'

I opened the door and the cold air rushed in, and turning to my wife I kissed her for the last time.

'Promise.' I reiterated.

'And hope to die ...'

They were be the last words I would ever hear her speak.

Chapter 22

   The snow was deeper in places and all the more perilous for that as I worked my way down towards where the road lay buried, and as breath-taking as the scenery was, I kept my eyes on the ground my staff guiding the way with quiet assistance.
The sky still looked heavy but was holding its own and I was thankful for that as it would be easy to lose track of one's surroundings, but it was torturous going until eventually I passed the two wooden posts that marked the end of the track and then I was out on the road.
The farmer had obviously been out and about as two deep ruts were cut cleanly in the snow which made my going exceptionally easier. The cold was penetrative despite my thick gloves and various layers, and as my breath puffed great white clouds into the air my heart beat a steady tattoo that seemed to sing, *Men-na, Men-na, Men-na...*
Far ahead a long trail of smoke rose up into the leaden skies and I increased my pace. It was the farmhouse. I was nearly there!
The dogs set up a cacophony of barking as I finally trudged into the snow-covered yard. They bounced and yapped furiously behind their enclosure as a door slammed somewhere nearby and then a small thick-set fellow strode into view his face half-hidden by a scarf beneath his cap.
'Bore da!' He cried coming towards me, 'What brings you here? Are you lost?' His pace faltered as he saw the size of me, before resuming his approach, but I sensed his sudden wariness as I did the excitement of the dogs.
I pulled off my hat and he stopped some feet away in perplexity as he now took in my face. It was the usual response, the tattoos coupled with my dark skin always elicited something of a shock at first sight.
'I'm Jonas Llewellyn, we're staying up in your hut ... forgive the intrusion but I'm afraid the bad weather has meant a change to our plans. Can you help get us out? The car is well and truly snowed in up there.'
The expression on his face went from astonishment to bemused recognition as he heard my Welsh accent that always sat so

incongruously with my exotic appearance, and then coming forward he gazed up at me curiously.
'Why Mr Llewellyn, you look done in, boy, of course I'll pull you out, but first come warm yourself and have a *panad.*'
I shook my head.
'Thank you, but no...I need to get back. My wife...she isn't feeling too good and well, I'd rather go straight away, if you don't mind.'
He nodded, a whole host of questions in his eyes, the most prominent and usually common one being who, or what exactly was I. But there was no time to be lost and he must've seen the urgency in my eyes.
Turning his head he bawled, *'Nerys!'*
A window opened from upstairs in the farmhouse as the farmer's wife stuck her head out.
'Be'?'
'I'm taking the tractor up to *cwt y bugail* to get the couple's car out!'
Her mouth dropped open as she saw me towering over her husband like a dark giant and in an uncertain tone raised her voice sharply.
'Be' sy'n digwydd, Gerwin? Is everything alright?'
'Iawn, iawn, we'll be back shortly,' the farmer turned back to me his eyes bright; 'you'll pop in and have a cuppa afterwards, won't you?'
The infallible hospitality of the Welsh! My heart was touched by his courtesy, but then seeing the speculation in his eyes, no doubt both he and his wife would be agog for gossip and an unexpected event in their day.
'That would lovely. *Diolch.*'
It was the standard reply, of course, and nodding his head he shouted back to his wife.
'Make sure you've got the kettle on, Nerys and some fresh eggs from the coop. We won't be long!'
I waited stamping my feet as he went to retrieve his tractor from the shed. The farm dogs were now regarding me in silence. Ears pricked forward, eyes bright.
I wondered if they'd heard the howling the previous night, and something about their demeanour told me they did. But they sensed even more with me and stood quietly as though awaiting some command.
I took advantage of the moment to fold my staff into its alternative

shape and slipped it over my neck taking care to keep the large cross hidden.

With much smoke and spluttering the tractor emerged from one of the barns just as the snow began to fall in earnest. I felt a rising tide of urgency and as with an unconcerned air the farmer ambled across to where I waited before gesturing I get in.

With great difficulty I squeezed myself into the cab and somehow managed to curl myself into a position so the door could be shut. Satisfied that I wasn't going to fall out the farmer then shifted gear and we pulled off.

The snow was continued to come down steadily as the tractor forged ahead at a sedate pace.

We made the journey in silence, the farmer concentrating on the task in hand as I mentally reached out across the snowy landscape to the shepherds hut and Menna.

I felt nothing, but then the cold, my anxiety, not to mention my fatigue had all worked to dull my senses. Usually finely-tuned they hummed and buzzed just beneath the surface as the thump of the windscreen wipers became almost hypnotic.

Of course she was there, I told myself. She'll be safe and warm and snuggled up before that fire without a care in the world.

'Can't we go any faster?'

The farmer gave me a wry glance and made a sweeping gesture with one hand.

'You can see how it is. Best we go steady, eh? Even this old girl can have a bad day if she's pushed too far.'

I didn't know what to say to that. Farmers for the most part were beyond my remit, but I respected their knowledge for the land and horse-power engines and so murmured an apology that was received with a brief nod.

After what seemed an age we finally reached the turning and I all but had to resist the urge to jump out of the cab and run up the track. I could see the deepness of my tracks from my sojourn down before the tractor swallowed them up, but already the snow had began to fill them in and I could only sway with the movement of the cab as the iron horse took us closer.

'*Duw, Duw*, this is bad, very bad....' observed the farmer with a

slightly concerned air, 'just a few light showers, the forecast said. Aye, well, for all their technology they still can't get the weather right, eh? But don't you worry we'll have you out in no time.'
It was an attempt to reassure me, I knew, but by now my whole being was wired up and fraught with an unknown fear that must in some way be transmitting itself to my kindly rescuer, and I barely acknowledged him as my eyes scanned frantically ahead.
From my elevated position I saw the snow-capped roof first as we came over the ridge and then as my heart flew into my mouth as I saw the door. It was standing wide open.
This time I didn't hold back and launched myself through the door and with such speed I only had time to hear the farmer emit a sound of surprise as I landed deftly in the snow before the tiredness in my legs took over and I staggered a few steps before the adrenaline kicked in.
I ploughed my way forward like a man possessed already removing the cross from my neck.
The farmer had pulled over and my inner eye caught a glimpse of him watching me open-mouthed as I headed for the open door my mind trying to deny what my eyes were telling me.
'She wouldn't have! She *couldn't* have! *She promised!*
My breath was coming in great gasps as I fought my way closer and an unbidden image flew across my mind of Menna relating the story of Gelert when Prince Llewellyn found the overturned crib ...
Snow had collected just inside the door and the woodburner was just a low glow as I stumbled in only to find the hut empty.
As I knew it would be.
'MENNA!'
My voice was strident despite feeling as though all the breath had been sucked from me and as I quickly checked the rooms at the back I heard a noise and turned to see the farmer stood in the doorway. His face was creased with concern.
'There, there, son, she can't have gone far.'
I stared at him but I wasn't listening. Then it came to me like a whisper on the wind.
The woods.

With a profound feeling of an impending tragedy I retraced my steps to the door as the farmer, seeing the look on my face respectfully stood aside.

Unerringly I turned and made my way down to where the tree line began and saw just the faintest prints that marked the passage of Menna's final walk.

I knew it as I knew the marks on my face, as I knew my own heartbeat and how it barely seemed to beat in anticipation of what I would find.

As I descended deeper the trees had become thicker, sentinels of an ancient land that silently watched me pass amidst the snow-filled hush.

My mind went to my father and how he had walked out into the desert that day never to return.

The cruelty that had befallen him. The mindless violence. The gracious acceptance of his fate and the intervention that had saved him.

Dare I hope for such mercy here?

Hope has a way of drawing us in like the sirens of old whose song would lure ships in and down to their doom. But there was no mercy to be found in these stark, cold woods and deep down inside I already knew the answer.

Menna was lying as though she was asleep. Curled up on one side, still dressed in her beautiful white gown. She looked like some fairytale princess cast deep in a trance. Her auburn tresses lay damp and gleaming on her bed of snow, a dying fire of the beautiful woman she once was, and in that moment the boy in me died forever.

Bending down I touched the cold cheek carefully as though afraid I might wake her. Her eyes were closed, the lips slightly parted as though about make answer, but she would never laugh or speak again, declare her love or call me Jonas *bach,* and throwing back my head I howled out my grief like a wild beast.

As the last of my cries echoed around the valley there came from the woods the wailing cry of a baby followed by a mocking laugh and in that instant I knew.

A lure had been set that would fool the kindest heart, and by some means dark and foul they had drawn Menna out from the cottage into the woods and down to her death.

With infinite gentleness I drew my beautiful bride of just one day into my arms and kissed the cold lips softly. Unseen eyes that bristled with spite watched me as I carried her back up through the trees and away from the snowy ground that had been her grave.

The farmer was still waiting in the doorway of the hut and I saw his eyes widen as he took in the sight. Removing his cap he murmured something in Welsh as I carried my wife for the second time over the threshold.

I laid my darling down on the couch and smoothed her brow before turning and facing my odd companion and sole witness.

'I'll leave you for a bit then, shall I...' he murmured awkwardly

I just looked at him. What more was there to say?

Everything had changed – forever. And in those moments I was a man far removed from rational thought and from God.

He nodded and closed the door behind him quietly.

I heard him start the tractor up and make his way down towards a world I would never look at in the same way again.

A world that is different for me because of who I am and the role I am expected to play in it.

I had thought to make my own rules and thwart the will of those who knew better; and for my own selfish desires my beloved had paid the price.

As I took her cold hands and laid them on my face, I wept and begged for her forgiveness. I prayed and I cursed, tormented by all the times we had spent together and knew in my heart I would never love another woman again.

This part of my life died on the snowy side of a mountain and showed me that there is evil in the world that exists purely to extinguish the light of our existence. But the dark forces made a mistake when they took my Menna. It's personal now, and therein now burns my passion, for I will hunt them down one by one for as long as God gives me breath in this body.

I was born in a hot dry country where my ancestors once hunted lions.

This is my story and you may take it as you will. For as I said at the beginning of my tale; nothing is ever as it seems, but this much is true ...

I am of an ancient tribe from the dawn of Time. A direct descendent of the first people who once walked this land - but the world is not ready for the likes of us yet, and so we work in shadow.

Legend says that our forebear, Simon the Sorcerer, came from Samaria. He did not.

Look to a cave in a place called Somerset. It sits not far from the holy site of Glastonbury where once the Druids held the most illustrious seat of learning throughout the Celtic realms, and know that this legacy and those of this bloodline live on.

My name is Jonas Llewellyn, and my journey is just beginning.

~ Welsh / English Translations ~

Bach – small, dear
Be' - *(abbr)* What
Be' sy'n digwydd – What's happening?

Cariad – love / sweetheart
Carfarchion – Congratulations
Croeso, dyn sanctaidd – Welcome, holy man
Cwtch – cuddle

Dewch chi mewn – come in
Diolch - Thanks
Duw – God

Heddlu – Police
Hiraeth – Longing
Iawn – alright
Iesu Grist – Jesus Christ

Llygad ysbryd – spirit-Eye
Llyn Tegid – Lake Tegid
Llys – Court

Mae'n iawn – It's alright
Nos da – Goodnight
Panad – cup of tea
Pob lwc – Good luck

Sospan fach – Little saucepan (song)
Trueni – Pity
Twp – Stupid

Wrth gwrs – Of course
Ynys Môn – The Welsh name for Anglesey

Printed in Great Britain
by Amazon